Dam Diligent

Dam Diligent

Book Two

IAN T. WALKER

PARTRIDGE

To order additional copies of this book, contact
Toll Free 800 101 2657 (Singapore)
Toll Free 1 800 81 7340 (Malaysia)
orders.singapore@partridgepublishing.com

www.partridgepublishing.com/singapore

Contents

Introduction ix

1 Dam and the Checkout 1

2 Dam and the Trapeze 7

3 Dam Trains as a Terrorist 13

4 Dam Lives in New York 23

5 Dam and the Bird 28

6 Dam's Solar Hot Water Heater 35

7 Dam's Tyres 42

8 Dam and the Washing Machine 49

9 Dam and the Tractor 56

10 Dam Builds a Helicopter 61

11 Dam Goes Pod Fishing 70

12 Dam Visits the Tip 82

13 Dam and the Caterpillars 89

14 Dam and the Vegetable Garden 95

15 Dam Diligent the Lion Tamer 101

16 Dam's Damn Dam 110

17 Dam Finds God..115

18 Dam goes Opal Mining.......................................121

19 Dam Goes Bushwalking 144

20 Dam Goes Pig Hunting 150

21 Dam Fights Fire..160

22 Dam and the Little Red Racing Car 166

23 Dam and the Butcher...172

24 Dam and the Christmas Tree.....................................176

25 Dam Writes a Letter 181

26 Dam Plays the Cello 189

27 Dam and the Apple Tree.......................................193

28 Dam Plays with Science 208

29 Dam Paints a Building...213

30 Dam and the Sky...224

This book is dedicated to the smiling faces
of Raphael, Ahryn and Chunli.

Introduction

Dam Diligent grew up in a city of asphalt where nature struggled to survive, crushed between cracks of metal and pavement. Despite these harsh surroundings, Dam discovered a talent for creativity and innovation. When his parents first gave him a skateboard, for instance, he found the little piece of wood on wheels too small, which is why he thought a limousine-sized skateboard would be preferable.

Dam Diligent is part one of a series written over fifteen years and encompassing over ninety short stories. Each story exposes the meek foibles of humanity with Dam at the center. The simplicity of day-to-day life, boring to some, only brews invention for Dam as he seeks to expand the minutiae of normal human existence.

He dyes his hair strange colors to stand out. He makes up words to keep things interesting. He explores deep, dark caves, but also the world at large. Dam is always inspired and sometimes ridiculous as he clings to the joys of youth and refuses to grow up. His life is one of discovery and escape as he discovers the wonder of being alive and escapes taking himself—or other people—too seriously.

1

Dam and the Checkout

When Dam was young he would often help his mother do the shopping.

His mother would spend hours in the supermarket talking to people and reading the labels on the food. And worse than that she would take so long at the checkout because there were so many people who all seemed slow and wanted to talk endlessly. Dam being diligent worked out how to speed his mother up. At first he would say he wanted to go to the toilet at the same time as the checkout girl was scanning the food and if that didn't work he would just run on through and disappear!

His mother knew what he was up to, after all he was always in a hurry to explore something new.

All the customers stopped to chat to the checkout girls who were so courteous and always asked the shoppers about their health. Some customers spoke for hours about their aches and pains and some said they were well even though they had trolleys of expensive food which was obviously not good for health as they looked very ill and overweight.

Dam was a small person and difficult to see side-on as he was so thin.

His mother had worried about him as a child and remembered that he was a pre-mature baby and born in an Angry-lance, which was Dam's word for 'Ambulance.' She understood his impatience, for immediately after he was born he stood up and said,

"Well I'll be damned! I thought I wasn't going to get out for a while!"

The Angry-lance driver couldn't believe his ears and told Dam's mother to buy a lottery ticket! The ticket won the lottery and Dam said,

"It's about time!"

Now that Dam was a little older he only went to the supermarket every two weeks. He lived in a small house and did the shopping on his own. However he still hated waiting in queues, it was the one thing which bored him and drove him quite silly. Spending money was a little like being born, he mused; the checkout queue a little like a birth canal and the till, like an obstetrics machine to whom one hypnotically gave one's life away. Then after breaching the opening if one didn't feel newly borne there was something wrong with you!

He would often dress up or down so he could be first served because if he was kept waiting he fall asleep instantly and had to be woken up. The checkout girls were fairly used to Dam and watched him with caution. Some even held up other customers to allow him through first. Even a five minute wait would make Dam slump over his trolley and begin snoring.

People would look at him horrified. He'd often end up flat on his back blocking everybody's way snoring and twitching with his dreams. And if one woke him up he'd sometimes snarl or bark like a dog and look at you as though you were an enemy!

He made a large funnel web spider from wood and plastic which he put on his head. He attached fine pieces of long hair to it and bits of wood which he put in his mouth so when he moved his mouth the spider's legs moved. Consequently he was speeded up at the checkout and when the checkout girl looked at him he'd blow his cheeks out which made the spider rear up.

Then he'd say in a serious tone, "Tame" or "she doesn't like waiting!" That was okay until a woman clobbered him with her handbag from behind and sent him sprawling into his trolley which banged into a chocolate stand and sent a packet of round sweets scattering across the floor. Luckily the spider fell dead in the trolley.

On another occasion he swallowed the wood and the spider suddenly came down onto his mouth where it hung between his lips. He quickly apologised and put it back on his head. But the checkout girl couldn't get away because she'd jammed her fingers in the till and nearly had a heart attack!

Yet again he went shopping in just a bath towel wrapped around his waist. He'd wet his hair in the carpark and told the checkout girl that he'd forgotten to buy soap. That day he bought his normal two weeks supply of food and kept everybody waiting as he searched for his money.

He had tried to inform the owners in a round-about way that other people too did not like standing in queues. He did this by filling his trolley to overflowing then saying he'd left his money in the car! Of course he would never come back.

He quite liked supermarkets. One thing which amused him was to sprinkle spaghetti all over the entrances to the aisles and then bark like a dog and watch all the attendants run around looking for the dog. People began slipping and sliding everywhere! One enthusiastic dog catcher crashed into the shelves of tomato sauce which smashed and made the place look like an accident zone.

Another favourite trick of Dam's was to skate on large tins of dog food.

It certainly made people keep out of his way.

However riding his trolley was the most exciting thing to do, now that he was an expert at it. He had found that if he stuck one leg out in front like the bowsprit of a ship, he could fend off people and other trolleys. The first time he did it he ended up with his face in the meat fridge and his leg in the cheese.

He emerged trailing a long line of sausages. The attendants said he could keep the meat and the sausages!

People who knew Dam, kept well out of his way and generally he was served first.

One day he was rummaging through his garden shed when he came across some sulphur. He remembered how years ago he'd mischievously lit some sulphur at his school and managed to evacuate not just his classroom but the whole school! Everybody went home early.

This afternoon he had to go shopping so he decided to take a little tin of sulphur along to the supermarket. He was looking forward to buying some lettuces and making lettuce sandwiches.

On the way up the ramp to the shop he noticed a man dressed in red with large boots on. He had a long white beard and a funny hat and was calling out,

'Merry Christmas!' and handing out pink ice creams. Dam liked ice cream so he took one. Dam licked it before he paid then couldn't find his money!

The supermarket was packed with people scuttling and pushing trolleys everywhere. All Dam wanted was three lettuces and a box of matches.

Dam charged through the entrance then backed out and took a lick of his ice cream. Then charged through again, then backed out and took another lick.

He did that three times! He liked to watch the lever barricade becoming confused. He would laugh outrageously at that making sure to show his bottom teeth to the onlookers!

He proceeded straight to the lettuces and took out his huge shopping list which went down to the floor. 'Matches' it said so he took three lettuces and pushed off. As he was sailing past the bread a small child ran out in front of him and was knocked flat by Dam's protruding leg. The poor child sat on the ground and cried. Dam tore some lettuce leaves off and blew the child's nose with them. He then gave the child his ice cream. The child's mother was huge.

Dam was sitting on the floor but he only came up to her knees!

"Oh, I'm, so sorry - Merry Christmas," was all he could say!

Dam came to the aisle with the matches in it so he took out his huge shopping list again. 'Lettuces' it said so he reached up and found a box.

He then unravelled his shopping list again and secretly opened the tin of sulphur and lit it on the floor under a pile of lettuce leaves. A little puff of foul smelling odorous smoke drifted up above his head and soon the air became putrid, though Dam of course could smell nothing.

He rode his trolley around and barked a few times. But nobody came running.

As he was speeding along his trolley suddenly stopped and he was propelled over the front of it on to the floor which he found was covered in spaghetti.

His shoes began to crackle and he found it very difficult to stand! When he approached the checkout he noticed many people holding their noses.

One checkout girl who had recently died her hair black and aged herself considerably, was waving the air frantically! Somebody had made a bad smell!

Then everybody began to run. Everywhere women were abandoning their trolleys and running out of the supermarket! Dam frowned and looked very worried as he squeezed passed a few trolleys. When he passed through the checkout he noticed the checkout girl had passed out with her nose in the till!

Dam said "Merry Christmas," and launched his trolley down the ramp. Santa Claus was still there, but he'd also passed out, head first in his ice cream!

"Merry Christmas" Dam said, trying not to breathe as he sailed past.

A little further on he only just squeezed past the large lady with the small child he had accidentally run over. He flew passed them broadside and crashed into the wall at the bottom of the ramp. The woman peered down at him and told him he was dangerous. The small child looked at Dam as though he was an enemy.

Then something changed in Dam and he left his trolley and ran back up the ramp and back into the supermarket. There was nobody around. He ran to the matches aisle and found his sulphur under the lettuce leaves and picked it up in the leaves and put it in his pocket and ran back down the ramp. But when he reached his trolley he turned again and rushed back up the ramp. He went to the drinking water aisle and took a bottle of water from the shelf. On his way out he poured water all over the poor checkout girl who still had her nose in the till. She quickly woke but did not see Dam as he was down the ramp doing the same to Santa Claus after removing his hat. Then he jumped in his trolley and launched himself outside.

In the carpark he found many people fanning themselves. He pulled the sulphur out of his pocket and burnt his fingers!

"Yeow!" he cried as he threw it in the trolley where it continued to fume and smoke. Everybody was stunned. Then Dam said,

"Well I'll be damned, I thought I wasn't going to get out for a while!"

To Dam's amazement they all cheered and clapped! Dam walked over to his little blue car, loaded the lettuces in and drove off. He wound all the windows down but it didn't really help.

When he arrived home he made himself a lettuce sandwich. He wished he hadn't as it tasted absolutely disgusting. And he couldn't get the sulphur smell out of his car for weeks!

2

Dam and the Trapeze

Many many years ago when Dam was a young man he decided to join the circus. Not because his legs were long or he could do funny tricks, he just liked watching the various acts people did. So one day when the circus was in town he went down to the manager's caravan and applied for a job doing something....anything!

He was delighted when the manager gave him the job of feeding and cleaning out the animal cages. There were lions to feed and he learnt how to roar, there were elephants to feed and Dam learnt to blow through his nose like an elephant, there were horses to feed and Dam learnt to talk to them in horse language. But best of all he was able to watch the circus many times for free.

Dam met new friends at the circus. He met the clowns and they made him laugh. He met the fat man with the water act, he made Dam feel a little ill and he met the ladies of the trapeze and they took Dam's breath away. He met the lion tamer and the elephant man. He became best friends with the horse trainer and his son and would often visit them and hear their stories about life in the circus.

Pretty soon Dam learnt a few tricks from the clowns and began to understand how the circus worked. As the days went by he discovered lots of things the public didn't know about each particular act.

For instance he learnt how the fat man was able to swallow a bucket of water and squirt it all back out again. He learnt how the trapeze artists timed their jumps and how the elephant trainer communicated with his elephants.

Dam learnt how to talk to them as well and they would answer intelligently as he scratched their nose.

Dam never saw himself as a performer; he was quite happy cleaning out the animal's cages and helping to put up the big-top tent which was huge. Everybody liked Dam, he seemed to do his work extremely diligently.

He always had a smile and a good word to say to everybody.

One day when the circus was in full swing, something went wrong during the elephant act. One of the elephant's collars had come loose and was becoming entangled in the animal's legs as it walked. On seeing this Dam jumped over into the ring and sprang upon the elephants front knee where he hung on like a monkey as the elephant hopped along on three legs. Dam held the crowd in suspense as he fixed the collar back up by springing onto the elephant's back after climbing up its ear. The elephant gave a loud trumpet because it liked Dam and Dam stood on its head and took a bow.

The audience clapped and cheered it was a very brave thing to do.

That evening the manager called Dam into his office.

"Do you think you could do that again?" he said. Dam went bright pink and said,

"No, I only like cleaning out the cages."

The following evening one of the clowns became ill and could not go on.

The manager was in a dilemma.

"What shall I do?' he exclaimed and looked at Dam. "Dam my boy," he said.

"Oh no!" said Dam.

"Oh please!" said the manager and added, "All you have to do is stand there!"

Dam was dressed up as a clown. He put a large red nose on and some white make up. He had a big smiling mouth and huge eyelashes. He was given some great big baggy pants and some huge shoes which were difficult to walk in.

The other clown looked at him and said he looked terribly funny.

Dam was scared. He picked up his broom and in they went but Dam fell over. As he was getting up the other clown grabbed his broom and hit him on the bottom with it so Dam fell over again! When he was getting up the clown poked him with the broom and he fell over again because of the huge shoes! Poor Dam felt quite silly and when he was getting up for the third time he moved aside and the broom missed him and the clown twisted around and fell over.

Now Dam was laughing. The other clown started chasing Dam around the ring with the broom. But Dam climbed up the trapeze ladder and took off his great big shoes and threw them at the other clown. Luckily they missed but one of them landed in the fat man's bucket of water.

Dam climbed higher and higher. The other clown ran around and around in circles with the broom between his legs. Dam grabbed the trapeze swing and took off. Something in Dam made him do six triple summersaults before he hit the net below. He bounced to the ground but the broom was upon him.

He jumped over it and ducked under it. He raced and grabbed his shoes and threw the bucket of water over the clown who chased him out of the ring.

The crowd was in hysterics, they loved it.

"Will you do it again?" said the manager.

"No!" said Dam. "I only like feeding the animals and cleaning the cages."

Several days later Dam was standing watching the horse act when something overcame him and he grabbed his broom and jumped up on one of the horses which was running around the ring. Taking his broom he placed it on the horse's saddle. He then climbed up and sat on it and began to clap.

Dam obviously possessed an extraordinary ability for balancing and the crowd cheered and whistled their applause.

"Will you do it again!" said the manager. "No," said Dam, "I only like cleaning the cages." The manager smiled and patted Dam on the back.

"You are a very diligent man" he said.

Several weeks later when they were pitching the tent in another town a hole appeared in the roof of it. It was Dam's job to mend the tents so he set about then and there to fix it.

"No time," said the manager. "We've got to put it up now."

"But it might rain!" said Dam looking at the grey clouds.

"We'll have to risk it!" said the manager and added that one day he might be able to afford a new tent.

The big-top tent went up and just as it did it started to rain. Dam went off to clean the cages and since it was raining he placed the wheel barrow full of elephant poo under the edge of the tent where it wouldn't get wet.

Dam went back into the tent and looked up at the hole. Rain was dribbling through it. A wind had sprung up and the big tent was blowing in and out.

Not many people came that night but those who did saw Dam Diligent at his best.

As the circus started and the show progressed, Dam was watching the hole in the big-top when a great gust of wind hit the tent. There was a tearing sound and everybody looked up. The hole was growing larger and it looked like the tent might tear in half! In no time at all Dam raced and fetched his needle and thread. With his needle in his teeth and the thread in his pocket he climbed up the trapeze ladder.

At that moment the elephant act was going on below him and though the act was good to watch it was not as exciting as Dam and the hole in the roof! Everybody watched as he climbed higher and higher. Just as he was near the top another great gust of wind hit the tent and the hole grew so large rain began to pour in.

Even the elephants stopped and watched Dam their trunks pointing up at their friend, huffing and puffing.

Dam climbed even higher than the ladder. In fact he walked out on one of the guy-wires which attached the ladder to the side of the tent. He had the trapeze in his hand. The thin wire he was standing on was bouncing up and down with the movement of the tent. He took a little run along the wire and sprang upon the trapeze.

Gradually he worked up the swing until he was close to the hole. Then all of a sudden he let go and disappeared out of the hole! The audience and the elephants gasped!

Where had he gone? The crowd became concerned as Dam did not appear. Suddenly there was a wet thud on the roof and people pointed saying,

"There he is!" and they all knew he had landed.

The crowd watched as he made his way back up to the hole. The wind was raging and the rain began to thunder down.

Then two hands appeared through the hole with a needle and thread.

The crowd held their breath as the needle went in and out and Dam went up and down with the wind. In no time at all he had stitched up the hole and the crowd stood up and cheered!

They watched as the bulge made by Dam's body slid down the outside of the tent and disappeared. Dam had saved the tent!

Things would have gone quite well for Dam had he not landed in his wheel-barrow of elephant poo. He came back into the ring cold and wet and covered in poo. The crowd seeing him leapt to their feet and cheered again. Fortunately the fat man was in the middle of his act and gave Dam a thorough washing down.

Dam took a bow and the crowd clapped and whistled.

Early the next day Dam was awakened by a knock on the door. It was the manager and all the circus performers. The clowns, the trapeze artists, the lion tamer, the fat-man and the elephant and horse trainers all stood outside his door.

"Dam," said the manager, "we all need to thank you for being so diligent and saving the big-top! And I'm not going to ask you to do it again because it won't happen again. Today I'm going to buy a new tent and here," he said handing Dam a new broom, "is a new broom with your name written on it."

Dam, feeling very bashful went bright pink and looked down at the broom.

It had the words "Dam Diligent the Magnificent Trapeze Artist" written on it.

3

Dam Trains as a Terrorist

One morning Dam decided to sweep the floor of his house before he had breakfast. He usually ate before doing the house chores but this morning - well, since he'd grown a little older, today had to be different. It wasn't long before great clouds of dust were billowing up in front of the broom. He hadn't swept the floor in years and his friends the ants had made piles of gravel and sand in one corner.

Dam lowered himself down to his knees and began rolling grains of sand off the ants little battlements and taking them over onto the small wall he was intent on building.

Dam was setting up a battle field. No sooner had he stolen their earth than they all came running out angrily and tried to scare him away. Dam soon forgot about sweeping he'd found a new game.

The ants were emerging from a hole in the floor so Dam being diligent rolled a large sand grain on top of it which prevented them from coming out. He had won the war. He stood up with his broom which had become his flag, saluted and his tummy rumbled.

Dam swept up his little battlefield and emptied the ant refugees outside.

He swept into the kitchen and had his breakfast. While he was eating he noticed a few ants on the table attacking his crumbs. Dam took a large spoonful of his breakfast outside and fed the refugees.

When he returned he switched the radio on for someone to talk to. He could talk to the man on the radio while he was chewing his food, the man didn't seem to mind.

The news came on and soon the topic changed to war. Dam reached over and turned it off. He'd been at war a long time ago and hated it. Everybody spent their time accusing others of misdeeds and it made Dam upset. That's why he lived a long way from other people with only himself to get angry with, with only himself to fear.

Just before he flicked the switch he heard the word "terrorists." It stuck in his mind over breakfast. He kept saying "terrorists" to himself and then changed the word to "territorialists." He thought about the ants and how they were terrorists living in his house, stealing his breakfast and defending "their" territory.

But then Dam was the terrorist because he'd disturbed them. He was as confused as the refugees he thought.

Dam suddenly felt very sad, he went back to bed. He remembered how long ago he'd trained in the hills of the Himalaya to fight the Merry-cans because they wanted to control an oil supply line and because they were big, greedy and clean shaven.

In those days Dam was ninety seven years old and his beard was down to his knees when he let it loose. Usually it was tied up in a bun above his head.

Dam had joined the Taliban movement in Afghanistan which was run by a man called Oh-my Beanladen. To gain entry into Beanie's camp all one had to do was grow a beard, read a book and sight a rifle. This was easy for Dam as he was the hairiest person on earth and it was easy for him to look at a rifle.

He couldn't read though, so he pretended to understand. Dam thought he'd be of assistance to the other terrorists since he had many ideas on how to distract people, the principle one being with the use of a mirror. Dam had found that it had great influence on people in general. For instance clean shaven men were intrigued by it while bearded men were often quite terrified.

Dam had been in A-Merry-car once, he knew how nice some of the people were. However he had no idea that his invention of the mirror, would have such an impact on their lives and he didn't like the way some Merry-cans still spent more time looking at themselves than planting beans.

Dam had used mirrors as a secret weapon during the war but he now disbelieved in them and mistrusted them because they could watch one if one wasn't careful and catch one unaware. More than once he'd been tricked into saying, "How do you do" to himself in a mirror. Dam believed it was their transfixing quality which was their inherent danger.

There were no mirrors in Dam's house now - they were all outside in his bean patch. He marvelled at how they kept the birds away especially the turkeys. He reckoned it was because they were so ugly they were frightened of themselves. In his bean patch Dam found the only friend he could talk to and who really listened. Not like the man on the radio who was always terribly busy.

Dam often had long conversations with the mirror. Sometimes he'd be a robber and say, "stick em up!" and at other times he'd be a saint and say "I am the way, the truth and what a sight!"

Dam's mirror was outside because he couldn't bear the thought of anybody watching him while he was asleep. He found he couldn't sleep with a mirror for every time he'd wake up he'd find someone watching.

Because Beanie was a wanted man, he lived in an underground palace away from the dust and heat. He had enough tinned food to last him a lifetime and people lowered beans and milk down to him each day through a long pipe which looked like an old tree stump on the top of the ground.

He'd been living there for so long his skin had turned white and all his hair had fallen out.

There was a lot of ammunition kept in the palace so when one went to see him it was totally dark as no candles or lights were allowed.

Dam had been making a large mirror in his tent for some months. He had assembled lots of glass and had found some special stones to melt from a high mountain to put on the back of the glass to make the reflective surface.

When his mirror was finished he showed it to a friend. The man let out an almighty shriek and passed out!

"I knew this would work!" said Dam. Next he placed the mirror at the end of a trench and watched the men as they came up and stood beside it. The men took no notice of their orders, they were transfixed. Some of them talked to it and after a while Dam found half the army poking their tongues out, laughing and pulling each other's beards in front of it. The men were horrified when Dam came and took the mirror back to his tent. They thought he had made them disappear!

Next day the commander came into Dam's tent and asked to see Dam's Weapon of Mass Destruction. When the man saw himself he fell to his knees and said,

"This is truly an evil thing! I love it! Oh-my must see this!"

Dam was blind-folded and led along a ridge top by his beard then down into some valleys and then under the ground through a tree stump. Dam found himself in a dark, cold smelly place. He was told to sit on the floor with his mirror beside him for Oh-my would be in shortly. Dam sniffed the air something was really bad.

It wasn't long before a man with a white face and shorts came and sat in front of him. All Dam could see in the dark was a pale white face and his little white legs.

"Oh!" said Beanie, "that is very b..beautiful!" and went away. Dam was led back to his tent by the beard. He was holding his nose and all he could say was,

"Oh-my Beanladen!"

Several days passed then one morning the commander entered Dam's tent.

"You're needed on the front line" he said. Dam picked up his mirror and was driven to the front line.

It was a hot day, the dust and the heat were added enemies. Dam was told to wait for the order to charge for they were going to try to overrun some Merry-cans who had dug in not far away. There were one hundred hairy troops ready to go with Dam and he sat down behind his mirror to await the signal.

All of a sudden he was off. He raced to the top of the ridge and ran on.

The mirror was extremely heavy and he could only carry it fifty paces before he had to put it down. Bullets were flying all around him. His friends were falling like flies. Dam picked up the mirror and ran on. He couldn't see where he was going and didn't know how far to go. He stopped again and looked back.

There were dozens of dead men behind him and only a few left standing.

The field looked like a moth-eaten carpet. Dam ran this way and that with his mirror but still the bullets kept flying and men kept falling. He ran on.

Then all at once the firing stopped. Dam sat down, he was exhausted. He had failed he thought because the Merry-cans weren't interested in looking at themselves at all! He could hear voices from up front and when he peeped around he saw all the Merry-cans with their helmets off standing in front of the mirror admiring their smooth chins and combing their hair!

Dam gasped, they were all so close, on the other side of the mirror!

"Damn!" he said as he realised he'd run all the way to their front line!

"Oh man, this is beautiful!" he heard one Merry-can say. Dam hid behind the mirror. He quickly began to dig a hole to cover himself with soil.

"Hey come and have a look at this!" said a Merry-can who had found Dam digging in the dust.

"Micky Mouse! This must be the hairiest Taliban I've ever seen!" With that Dam and his mirror were captured.

The Merry-cans loved the mirror but no matter how hard they tried, Dam would not tell them how he'd made it. He soon realised why they were called 'Yanks' because they kept yanking his beard. Dam wasn't impressed when they called his mirror 'their' secret weapon of mass erection.

That night Dam lay in a locked room. He looked out the window at the steely blue stars and wondered if he'd ever sleep in his tent again. As he lay on the ground in the cold dry air he was sure he could hear faint scratching sounds. Maybe it was oil flowing through a huge underground pipe. No, it seemed to be getting louder and louder until all of a sudden the ground began to mound up and move. Dam stood back as out of the ground came a Taliban with shovels strapped to his hands. He had a white face and spindly white legs.

"D..D..Diligent, I presume?" he said. In no time at all Dam jumped into the hole and was led through a network of underground passageways by his beard. The man with the shovels repaired the hole in the floor and was taking Dam back to his tent.

Next day the commander came into Dam's tent again and said that he would have to die as he'd lost himself to the Merry-cans. However if Dam made another mirror and used it to hijack an aeroplane in A-Merry-car then he would be spared.

Dam set to work making another mirror. He collected some glass and journeyed to a distant mountain to melt more rocks for the reflective backing. He made a small mirror so he could take it aboard the aircraft.

Dam was sent to A-Merry-car and there he met his fellow hijackers. Everybody was amazed at the beauty of the mirror and believed that it would sufficiently entrance the pil-ot into doing exactly what they wanted. The plan was to overtake the crew of the aircraft with the mirror and then put it in front of the pil-ot. Dam didn't understand why.

On the day it was all meant to happen Dam woke late. He was sleeping in a soft bed in a tall building with sheets and he couldn't sleep until he'd turned the mirror away. When he woke he had to race to catch the plane. He hadn't heard the other hijackers early morning phone call. He phoned for a taxi and that came late as well. He had to wait ages for the lift to come up to his floor and then he got out of it on the wrong level! His shoelaces would not do up properly and his beard was out of control due to all the strange smelling soap he'd used in the bathroom though somehow he managed to hide the mirror in his beard.

When the taxi dropped him at the airport all the people were already on the plane. Dam looked out across the airport with his Taliban eyes. He noticed a luggage car heading out towards the plane. As quick as a flash he dashed down the stairs and leapt over a very high fence. With blinding speed he raced over to a shed and found a loose wheel. Dam being diligent sent the wheel rolling and crawled inside. He rolled over towards the luggage car. When he was close to it he leapt out and clung onto the side of the vehicle. As the luggage was being loaded on the plane he wondered how he was going to get inside the aircraft without being noticed. But then he thought it would be better to be on the outside of the aircraft so he could show the mirror to the pil-ot through the window.

Dam let out a sigh as he saw that there were no hand grips on the outside of the luggage compartment door of the plane. As his luggage car began to move off he was taken past one of the aircrafts wheels. He leapt off and like a hairy spider climbed up the wheel and hid in the wheel housing.

Slowly very slowly the aeroplane began to move down the runway.

Dam clung on tight and the mirror did not move. Faster and faster they went and Dam could see the ground speeding below him. With a great rush of wind the huge wheels left the ground and he was airborne. The plane began to climb and Dam began to inch his way closer to the doors. Then the wheel began to move up into his space. Instinctively he fell onto it and manoeuvred to its underside. As the doors of the wheel compartments began to close he grabbed an edge of a door and flung himself to the outside of the plane. There he hung from one hand for an instant as his door closed. Unfortunately it closed on his fingers. Quickly he pulled them out and was flung back a little before he found a convenient hand-hold just forward of a light fitting.

Dam clung on like a leech. His eyelids were fluttering like umbrellas and he had to keep his mouth shut or his cheeks would blow out like a parachute.

He hung there a while until he worked out what to do. If he could climb up to the windows he thought he might be able to work his way along to the front of the aeroplane.

Dam took his shoes off and let them fall. He took his shirt off and then his pants. He stripped right down to his underpants to lessen the wind resistance.

A sudden chill went through his body as he felt the cold wind. With his diligent toes he found a small grip. Then he planted his barely controllable lips on the plane and sucked hard. Using his mouth he was able to glue himself to the outside of the plane like a sucker-fish or a giant leech.

Slowly very slowly he manoeuvred himself up to the windows and planted himself on a window with his lips. Then he stuck his fingertips into minute cracks and his diligent toes followed.

Each window had passengers behind it and Dam tried to give each a nice smile but the wind kept playing havoc with his lips so he fluttered his eyelids and blew his cheeks out like a parachute before scarily planting them on the glass. Then he would arch his body and move forward.

After quite some time he had advanced to within a few metres of the cockpit. His mirror was still in his hair and he was almost there. The only problem was his lips had swollen to three times their normal size and they had turned blue with cold.

Finally when he looked in the cockpit window he saw a very strange sight. The pil-ots, for there were two of them, were very peculiar looking people indeed. Dam had never seen faces like them before and he wondered if they weren't a special breed or race for they had strange eyes and huge swollen necks!

"Pil-ots!" he wondered as he produced the mirror. Immediately the pil-ots took their rhomboidal stockings off their heads and revealed themselves as Dam's fellow hijackers! On seeing the mirror they began to wave at themselves, to smile and show their teeth. But then they began to wave at Dam as though they wanted him to move away. But they soon stopped to look at themselves again and adjust their beards.

This was all too much for Dam who had begun to shiver uncontrollably in the cold. Under great pressure his huge blue lips became unstuck and his fingers lost their grip, the wind caught him and he was flung back along the length of the aircraft but he was held back! Dam's beard became entangled in the tail light and he was rudely stopped! He began to flap along behind like a fly on a string.

After spinning round and round he steadied himself with his arms out like a bird. With difficulty he pulled himself up to the plane with his beard and gripped the flashing light. He swung himself up and straddled it with both legs. His bare skin stuck to the glass and there he flashed like a fire-fly.

With his beard streaming out behind and his ears flapping in the wind, his huge blue lips were hard to keep closed. After a short while he could smell something burning! In a flash he realised his nylon underpants had stuck to the light! He suddenly began to feel burnt! He threw himself backwards and in an instant the plane left him.

He was falling. As he fell he caught the sight of the plane which seemed to be heading straight for a tall building. Then he saw it hit the building and burst into flames.

Dam hit some water. He had opened his mouth to act like a parachute.

He hit the water pretty hard. He had landed in a swimming pool which was on top of another building. When he came to the surface of the water he saw a lady in a bikini watching the burning building. Dam climbed out of the pool very quietly and covered himself with the mirror. He hid behind a wall and peeped around the corner. All he could think of was what the Taliban would do to him if they found out he had made the plane crash into a building! The woman turned around and caught Dam's eye hiding behind the wall.

"Eek!" she cried picking up a book. She yelled that she was a crack shot and if he didn't come out from behind the wall she'd brain him with the book!

Dam didn't like the sound of that so he stepped out, still hiding behind the mirror.

"Where the hell did you come from?" asked the woman.

"Oh!" said Dam fearing the book, "I dropped out of the sky!"

The lady looked at his lips then down at the mirror, Dam's secret weapon, and exclaimed,

"Oh isn't it beautiful!" Dam stood there dripping wet, he suddenly felt instantly warm, in fact he went bright red, as red as the flames. He looked into her eyes and felt his passion beginning to rise!

Dam never went back to the Taliban. He'd found something special to keep himself occupied. He shaved his beard off and made a carpet out of it and stayed in New York for many years where he started a business selling mirrors in the shape of hearts.

4

Dam Lives in New York

When Dam was in New York he lived in a little house in a normal street.

He had a normal letter box and a normal front lawn. And to make things even more normal Dam had a lawn mower which made a loud noise especially on Sundays. Dam loved mowing the front lawn, it was so easy. The ground was flat and the grass never grew above ten millimetres because he mowed it so consistently.

Dam fed the grass dog poo which he collected from the neighbourhood.

He was often seen with his little wheel-barrow shuffling along the street collecting it. He used to encourage the animals to come and use his front lawn as a toilet.

To help attract them he had built a large cat out of an old upside down garbage tin and made a head for it out of an old upside down bucket which he decorated with eyes, nose and whiskers. It even had ears which he'd made out of old carpet. He stuck coconut-fibre all over it as fur. It didn't really attract dogs, even though the grass mysteriously died all around it.

Dam found the best thing to attracted dogs was his old black brief case. So he drove a stake in the middle of the lawn and tied the case to it. Next day to Dam's delight there was dog poo all over his lawn. He ran about with his specially designed barbeque tongs and picked it all up and put it in a composting contraption he kept at the side of his house. This was full of a rare species of worm with had extendable jaws. They loved dog poo and purred like kittens whenever they were fed.

Dam would take the slurry from this composting contraption and sprinkle it on the front lawn using an old watering can. The grass would immediately stand up and grow, grow, grow!

All Dam's neighbours were jealous of Dam's lawn. The neighbour from the back had borrowed Dam's barbeque tongs once and mentioned that they were great for sausages and that Dam should patent them.

"That is the greenest lawn in the street," remarked the man.

"Ah," said Dam, "I'll show you my secret." They both went around to the side of the house and lifted the lid of the worm-box. The worms all came to the surface and began gnashing their teeth and purring. Dam gave them a stir with the tongs. He looked up but his neighbour had disappeared.

Dam enjoyed mowing the lawn. It was the only bit of exercise he did and consequently his legs and arms were as strong as steel. He'd often miss sleep on the Saturday night before, just thinking about how he was going to enjoy mowing the lawn the next day! He would even dress up for the occasion and wear a green outfit with a bright yellow hat and pink socks.

One Sunday morning he was feeling particularly elated and after a furious battle with the lawn mower to get it started, he revved it extra loud and long so vast plumes of white smoke surrounded his house. Half way through the mowing process two old ladies walked by and stopped to stare at Dam.

He was behaving most peculiarly. For while he was mowing he began to think of an excellent method for attracting more dogs to his lawn. He thought that if he learnt their language and called them in, then he could tie a string to the gate and close it behind them. Another string could open the lid of the brief case and reveal all the dog food he'd put inside. Dam would then keep the gate closed for several days and make the dogs feel at home by talking to them in their own language!

"What a fantastic idea!" he said to himself and immediately began barking like a dog. He pretended he was a large dog and a small dog having a conversation together so he was doing large low note barks then high pitched barks in reply. Dam was completely carried away by his doggie conversation and didn't notice the two old ladies watching.

Then Dam did a very strange thing, he started dancing! The lawn mower was singing away and Dam was pushing it with one hand and then the other as he kept barking and whining. At one stage he left the lawn mower roaring and raised his leg several times over the brief case. The ladies looked at each other.

Then Dam began to growl. He had a vicious attack with himself and was about to put his shoe in his mouth and thrash it from side to side but he was approaching his turn and with the deft precision of a ballerina he executed a flawless pike and tuck as he swung the mower around. A few quick double shuffles and some wiggles of the hips then,

Bang! Straight into the cat! Dam was violently flung over its coconut-fibre body and landed head first in the grass on the other side. Somehow before that happened he'd pulled the mower towards him and managed to run over his foot!

Dam let out an agonising scream and the ladies raced through the gate.

Dam's foot was still in its shoe on the other side of the cat but it was no longer connected to his leg! He tried to wiggle his toes but he'd cut his foot off!

Luckily the two women were there and they both knew exactly what to do. One woman pulled a plastic bag out of her handbag which was half full of beans and grabbed the barbeque tongs and picked up Dam's foot and put it in the bag.

The other woman raced inside and phoned an angry-lance (which was Dam's word for 'ambulance'). She found the kitchen and from the fridge grabbed a large container of ice-cream.

Outside the other lady had wrapped Dam's leg up tightly and made him lie down. He went as white as the ice-cream as the woman stuffed it around his foot in the plastic bag. The other woman found the watering can and gave Dam a drink. Then they all sat on the lawn and ate the rest of the ice-cream. Meanwhile the hungry lawn mower kept roaring beside them.

Dam had a dream. A woman in white robes was bending over him, she had big yellow eyes and very long canine teeth. Her breath was rank and her tongue was long and pink. She leant forward and with Dam's barbeque tongs grabbed his nose!

Dam woke up. He was in horse-piddle (hospital). There was a woman in white robes who leant over him and jammed a thermometer in his mouth.

Dam tried to talk but he swallowed the thermometer! He was whisked off on a flying bed which had little nasty wheels like a lawn mower.

Dam had another dream. He was perched in a tree dressed as a yellow bird. He was looking down on a green lawn, he recognised it. Suddenly lawnmowers began to attack him from the sky. They had wings and were flying at him like mad wasps. Dam started barking like a dog. And then to his surprise there was a huge cat in the tree on another branch. It lunged at him and knocked him out of the tree!

Dam woke up. There was a docked-door (doctor) looking down at him.

The docked-door had one normal eye and the other was like a sun. It came closer and Dam's heart began to leap about. The docked-door said something which sounded like a lawnmower. Dam closed his eyes again and fell into a deep green space.

Several weeks later Dam was at the local shopping centre on one crutch pushing a trolley around, buying some groceries. His foot had been sewn back on complete with its shoe, pink sock and a few beans. He didn't dare look down the aisle which had all the dog food.

In fact Dam's life had changed quite a bit since his accident. He didn't like his lawn mower anymore. He'd given it to the neighbour. His lawn was a metre high when he arrived home from the horse-piddle so he employed someone to come and dig it all out!

He had found something more suitable to plant instead of lawn and that was rocks... rocks, stones with sand in between - plenty of nice round rocks.

He kept the dogs away with a new invention which was a locked gate.

He enjoyed his new front garden sometimes by just sitting on one of the stones.

Dam pushed his shopping trolley outside. Climbed into it with all his shopping and pushed off down the hill. To stop himself he would open his umbrella out the back to slow himself down. He made sure he never crashed into any dogs by keeping his crutch out in front. Fortunately the run to his house was straight down hill and he reckoned he'd attained speeds in excess of one hundred kilometres an hour which was faster than any dog.

It gave Dam great pleasure to be normal. He often enjoyed sitting in the front yard watching out for dogs and loading his rock-throwing tongs which were quite deadly at one hundred paces. He often thought about how he could be even more normal, than normal.

After sometime he started a lucrative new business repairing windows.

5

Dam and the Bird

Dam loved birds. He often whistled back to them when he was in his garden. He didn't like to see them in captivity and if he could he would let them out whenever he saw one in a cage.

During his stay in New York he worked in an old nursing home cleaning the floors. He'd worked out a novel method of mopping them by tying mops to each foot and skating about the rooms. He would then stick each foot in the mop bucket and squeeze the water out using the spring lever on the side of the bucket.

Everybody loved Dam, he was a happy person, always whistling and saying hello to everybody. Everybody that is except the old lady in the hall who always sat next to a small table on which there was a cage with a very grumpy bird in it. The bird was some rare species from Africa. It had beautiful blue feathers.

The woman was always dressed in blue too and no matter how much Dam said hello to her - as he always did, she never looked up and never said hello back, probably because she was an old bird herself.

Dam didn't like to see the bird in the cage looking grumpy and often whistled to it in bird language. No reply.

When Dam had first started the work as a cleaner in the home he had attempted to move the cage in order to clean around it. The floor underneath was covered in seed as well. The woman had a walking stick and wacked Dam on the legs when she saw him about to move the cage.

"Don't you move that cage, don't you even touch it!" she said looking up at the apparition of Dam, her eyes suddenly looking twice as large. Dam smiled and kept mopping around the table.

The woman had been in the nursing home for ages. She had no family or friends only the bird. Her bed was opposite a door in the hallway near where she sat in her chair and often slept. She seemed to command considerable power over the staff for she was always demanding her food on time and if it was not fresh or too cold she had something to say. The bird was as messy as she was and only ate when she did, cracking its seed and splashing water on the floor.

The whole building knew when this woman was asleep as she snored like a bull. The very walls would vibrate and the door on the bird's cage would rattle.

One day when the building was shaking, Dam tip-toed up to the cage and tried to open the door. The bird seemed to be sleeping too. Just as he was taking the peg off the door, somebody came around the corner. Dam was startled and let the door bang back down. The bird woke up and stared beady eyed at Dam. The woman grunted and stretched her legs out.

"What are you doing?" said the woman who had come around the corner.

"Don't touch the cage!" came a familiar voice.

Dam looked down and said,

"Nice bird" and was about to walk away when he slipped in a pool of water and ended up on the floor along with the many husks of seed. The blue lady watched Dam suspiciously and demanded a cup of tea.

Over the next few weeks Dam became determined to let the bird out of the cage, after all it looked so miserable. So one day when the building was shaking again Dam peeped around the corner and waited till the coast was clear.

Quick as a flash he raced up to the cage but as he did the woman stretched her legs across and blocked the corridor. Dam seeing them just in time took a leap and collided with the other wall.

"Don't you touch the cage" came a familiar voice as he nursed an injured hand.

Dam forgot about doing such mischievous things as opening the door of the cage, he decided the woman could maybe see even as she slept. He kept skating around her legs with his mops and stopped talking to the bird.

One day a 'docked-door' as Dam called doctors, came to visit the lady.

He was giving her some pills saying they would stop her sleeping so much. Dam wasn't there at the time so he didn't see the docked-door drop a pill on the floor. It rolled under the small table and hid amongst the seed husks. Next day when Dam was cleaning the floor, he found the pill and popped it in the bird's water. The bird looked sideways curiously at its water and then up at Dam.

"Don't you touch that cage" said the lady. Dam replied saying,

"Looks a bit sick, needs to have some vitamins, maybe a bit of exercise!"

The woman picked up her walking stick and was about to poke Dam in the chest.

"You keep away or you'll go in the cage too!" she growled.

The woman stayed awake all day peering up at the ceiling then down at the floor then over to the bird. The bird began to walk backwards and forwards along its perch and look sideways at the woman and then down at its water.

Then an amazing thing happened the bird began to talk!

"Don't touch the cage!" it said over and over again as it bobbed up and down. The woman couldn't believe her ears and began to laugh. And then the bird began to laugh! People came from all around and watched as both of them were cackling away. Then a very peculiar thing happened, the bird suffered a stroke and fell head first in the water container. Dam raced up with his mops on his feet sliding to a halt in front of the cage and began to struggle with the door to open it.

The woman yelled at him and began to rain blows down upon him with her walking stick. Dam was struck many times on the head and arm. Several people restrained the lady as Dam thrust his hand in the cage and rescued the bird.

He pulled it out examined its eyes and put its body to his ear to see if it was still alive. Then to everybody's amazement he put its beak in his mouth and blew a little and gave it mouth to beak resuscitation.

"Ah he's eating it!" the woman screamed. Gradually the bird's eyes opened and Dam put it back on its perch. It looked shaken, wet and startled and eyed Dam with horror as he lowered the door and put the peg in his pocket.

"Don't touch the cage!" came a familiar voice. Dam squelched off with his mops, his own heart beating a little more quickly.

Several days later the woman was again asleep in the daytime and her snoring was very loud. Dam peeped around the corner and saw that the bird was still awake. He tip-toed up to the cage, lifted the door up and secured it with the peg. He woman grunted but did not move. The bird walked to the end of its perch and looked at the space where the door had been

Much to Dam's disappointment it did not fly out. In fact it seemed to fear the door being open and kept at the end of its perch.

"Poor thing," thought Dam. "It is really trapped." He looked at the woman snoring and thought the peg would be better off on the woman's nose.

As the days passed the woman didn't even notice that the door of the cage was open. The bird still stayed on its perch cracking its seed and drinking its water. Dam went into the kitchen and sprinkled a little bit of bird seed on her mashed potato. She ate it without noticing and began snoring again.

Dam sailed by on his mops and the woman lashed out at him with her walking stick. For some reason she didn't like Dam and she was often telling other people off too.

Dam decided to let the bird out - to let it know its freedom. He set about making an artificial bird out of a pair of blue socks. He found some feathers and stuck them in the end of it, he made a head and painted some eyes on it and a beak out of a shell. It was ready.

One day when Dam had finished mopping the hallway the woman dozed off with the bird. Both of them were asleep. Dam tip-toed up with his fake bird and put his hand in the cage and mounted it on the perch. The real bird woke up and began to flap its wings. Dam grabbed it with both hands and stuffed it down his shirt. He was just about to turn and run when an almighty blow from the walking stick momentarily blinded him. He staggered back and fell. Unfortunately for Dam he slipped on his mops and landed head first in his mop bucket! The jaws of the squeezing apparatus jammed shut about his neck and he sat up and drenched himself with water going everywhere.

The bird escaped. The woman shrieked and began to beat the air with her stick. Dam fought with the spring lever as several blows clanged on the bucket with a deafening sound. People came to his rescue. The bird flew about and landed on its cage. But the woman thinking it was trying to attack her bird which was really Dam's fake one, hit her bird with the stick and knocked it onto the ground where it lay in a pool of water its wings spread wide as though it was dead!

Dam was freed and sat on the floor. He indicated to all those around that they were not to talk about the dead bird on the floor. He bent down and picked it up without the lady noticing and put it in his shirt.

"Don't touch the cage!" came a familiar voice.

Dam took the bird to a safe place and everybody gathered around to look at it.

Poor Dam was very distressed and held it to his ear to listen for its heart.

And remarkably it was not dead. He examined its wings and found that one had been broken. He took the bird home and bandaged its wing. He let it live in his kitchen until its wing was better.

Meanwhile the blue woman had begun to look strangely at her stuffed socks in the cage.

"He's dead!" she said. "He's gone! He's not eating! He looks very sick!"

Several days later the woman passed away in her sleep. They all knew something was wrong when the building stopped shaking.

Dam was sad that she had died. He took the bird into the nursing home on his shoulder. Down the same corridor with the same table but no blue lady.

Dam now whistled to the bird and it seemed happy for it whistled back. He took the cage home as the bird had nowhere to sleep and eat and he knew the bird liked the cage as well as Dam's kitchen table.

The bird had found a friend at last and everybody in the nursing home talked to it. Dam would mop the floors with the bird on his shoulder. One day as they were both mopping the corridor at the spot where the lady and the bird had lived for so long, the bird said in a clear sweet voice.

"Don't touch the cage," and then made a very strange noise like snoring.

One day Dam was cleaning the cage when he found there was an extra bottom to it. Someone had made a small compartment beneath it. He opened it and to his dismay it was full of money! There was lots of it.

Dam did not know what to do. He sat down and counted it. He had never seen so much before! He looked across at the bird and whistled and the bird looked sideways at the money then up at Dam.

Soon after that Dam found himself in the bank. He and the bird were putting some money in Dam's account. All of a sudden the bird said,

"Stick em up!" Dam laughed. The lady behind the counter laughed too.

"Don't touch the cage." came a familiar voice then a strange noise like snoring.

6

Dam's Solar Hot Water Heater

It had been raining now for three days and Dam was feeling a little ragged and shot through like a shower nozzle, spegitified and draining. The morning was dreary and uneventful so to cheer himself up he went out to his garden to talk to his wet flowers.

The cabbages did not say much, they were tormented by caterpillars who seemed to be having religious gatherings around the stems. And the tomatoes were busy making umbrellas for the beetles who were entertaining the worms who in turn were entertaining a whole lot of flies while talking to a small wet lizard.

Nobody seemed to want to talk to Dam, they were all too busy. So he went and sat amongst his daffodils who were still waiting for the early morning bees. While they waited they sang a one word song as they bobbed their heads expectantly towards the sun and that one word song was 'be-you-tear-full!'

As dam was learning the tune and beginning to bob his own head in time, the phone rang. He raced inside. It was his friend who said he had a large dish of strong material which would make an excellent solar water heater for generating electricity from steam power or hot water for a shower and if Dam was interested to come and pick it up. Dam's inventive mind began to fizz, pop and sparkle!

"Oh, yes!" he said as he sniffed the perfume of new ideas.

Dam being diligent went about obtaining the dish from his friend's house in an unusual way for it was heavy and concave like a large bowl. He used it first as a boat and then as a large umbrella to transport to his house. He had no choice as it was too large and awkward to roll along the road.

When he arrived at his friend's house it began to rain hard. The small stream nearby soon became larger until Dam could stand it no longer, he was off.

He loved shooting rapids and swimming - he was truly amazing on a surfboard. He gave up surfboard riding after swallowing a blue-bottle stinger whole, but that was another story.

Dam was into the rapids as quickly as they were flowing. His friend helped him carry the dish down to the creek which was in moderate flood. He stepped inside it and was soon out in the strongest current.

The first obstacle was a barb wire fence! Dam was very lucky; he just fitted under it! Then he bounced off a few trees, turned a right angle and left the main stream entirely and found himself floating across a paddock! He soon lost control and went over a steep embankment, then hard left down another slope and back to the main stream! Somebody beeped the horn of their car when they saw him floating over the paddock.

Dam was sitting cross-legged in the bottom of the dish with his head just above the rim. He could stand up in it and make it move the way he wanted, however that was a little dangerous.

Not far ahead, his small creek was about to merge with a larger stream and Dam knew there was a small waterfall to negotiate before he joined the larger waterway. Just before the waterfall was a calm deep pond. Dam spun around and around for a minute getting giddy. He was wet through - the rain was still thundering down. He lay back and bailed a little with a bucket and peeped over the side.

The waterfall was close so Dam stepped out onto the shore and tried to manoeuvre the dish above the rocks. However something caught it and in an instant it turned up sideways to the stream and effectively plugged the top of the waterfall!

"Dear me" said Dam, "this will never do." In the pouring rain he jumped out into the rising water and felt the bottom edge for the obstruction but there was nothing there. The shape of the dish was preventing it from righting itself and the stream was getting deeper. In an inkling Dam was on the top of it like a sailor trying to right his yacht and quickly it rolled underneath him and scooped him up like a ball in a dish. Together they slid down the waterfall and down to the larger stream with Dam furiously bailing.

"This is the life!" said Dam, even though he was thoroughly wet!

After travelling for some time he came ashore and had to carry the dish on his head like a large hat or umbrella. It was too large and awkward to roll along the road so he had to walk in the middle.

He collided with parked cars and several trees for he couldn't see where he was going! He had to ask many people's feet, as he couldn't see their faces, the direction to his house. When he arrived home he found the dish didn't fit through the front door.

Over the next few weeks Dam spent many hours installing his dish on the roof of his house. He found a small water tank and bought some copper pipe. He was going to line the inside of the dish with mirrors and make a solar water heater.

Dam raised it onto his roof with a crane he'd made from three trees and a long rope which he tied to his car to lift the dish up. Then one overcast day he filled his invention with water.

Dam could not believe how efficiently it heated the water even on a cloudy day. The following day was sunny and after one hour of full sun the water in the tank began to boil! But Dam had forgotten to put a release valve on the top of the tank and just when he remembered there was an almighty explosion and the small tank shot twenty meters into the sky! Boiling water showered the trees and a great cloud of steam rose from the roof. After the tank crashed back to earth and the dripping and hissing ceased Dam, though a little shocked, was delighted with his new toy. He modified the design slightly and installed a release valve he'd made from a brick and a spring.

Soon after with the full sun on it the pressure release valve soon blew open and a fifteen meter jet of steam shot into the air with a high pitched deafening scream which became worse as the pressure increased. Dam ran around with his fingers in his ears. He was excited to see that it made so much energy and that night Dam had a plan.

Being the resourceful person that he was he decided to utilize the excess steam and use it to power a steam turbine. He had so many ideas he literally had steam coming out of his ears! He also decided to convert his washing machine into a steam engine!

The next day he lit a fire in his washing machine as an experiment. Then he fashioned a chimney and a better lid and a few more pipes in and out to carry the steam past the propellers which he'd fixed to the wheels. The excess steam from the two systems he thought could go through a flexible pipe which he'd buried in the front lawn. The steam from this pipe he hoped would be enough to power an electric turbine.

The water which fed the solar heater came from his fifty thousand gallon water tank which he used for the house. And the fuel for the fire in his washing machine steam engine was black coal which came from a hole in his backyard which he'd been digging for a fair while. But then Dam realised he did not need to light a fire in the washing machine as he had more than enough steam already from the solar heater to power it!

He climbed into the tub of his washing machine. Peeping over the rim of it he could just see where he was going. He was eager to try it out though it didn't have any steering as yet.

Dam designed a tracking system, powered by steam, which would enable his solar heater to follow the sun and position itself to the correct angle of the sun's rays.

Eventually he decided to mount the generator turbine up on the roof closer to the water heater and to narrow the feeder pipe into the generator for maximum efficiency.

He cut the rotor of the generator in half and hollowed it out in a spiral so the steam went through the middle of it. Then he attached more pipe to the end of the flexible pipe which went to his steam engine down on the ground. Alongside the generator on the roof he built a small level space for easy access.

He was angling the device into the sun for a trial run when quite suddenly he was thrown to one side by the guidance system and the turbine began to spin. Unfortunately the tracking system under the dish locked into its rotational axis and since Dam thought it would only turn slowly he had not included any kind of brake. Dam found that not only did it spin around fast but it began to roar like a rocket!

Dam leapt onto the platform and looked at it with amazement as it began to pick up speed and spin faster and faster. He began to think it might take off like a steam powered flying saucer!

In no time at all it began spinning wildly and shaking the whole house! Dam with his fingers in his ears began to fear for his life!

Just then a police car pulled up and two policemen leapt out and signalled Dam to climb down which he did. The policemen got out their guns and began to shoot at Dam's invention. But it picked up speed and began to roar even louder!

"Don't shoot!" cried Dam.

"How do you stop it!?" they cried.

Dam said the sun would go down in about five hours' time!

"Why are you shooting?" shouted Dam.

"Because we can't hear you!" they cried.

All three watched as the dish began to pick up speed and emit a high pitched scream. Dam climbed into his steam engine with his fingers in his ears! Eventually he relented and shouted that they would have to shoot the water pipe on the top of the dish. One of the policemen stepped forward and took aim.

Now fate has it that sometimes strange things happen and whether that bullet hit the water pipe or not will never really be known, anyway the following is the truth.

After he fired the bullet it ricocheted back and knocked the policeman's hat off his head! Then all of a sudden Dam's front lawn exploded as the flexible hose disconnected from the steam engine and leapt out of the ground hissing and spitting boiling hot water and steam everywhere!

The startled policemen jumped a metre in the air and momentarily stopped watching the solar heater and began shooting at the hose!

At the same time with a great crash the dish on the roof broke free and took off. They watched as it quickly rolled sideways and ran full-pelt along the roof where it hit the ridge and leapt ten meters in the air! It then hit the ground on its side and spun off down the street at an alarming rate!

One policeman fired a few shots again at the hissing pipe and the other grabbed his hat and together, still jumping about on funny legs, they charged off down the road chasing the screaming dish!

Dam looked on in silent disbelief from inside his washing machine.

Then a moment later from the side of his house three dogs appeared with their tails between their legs running as fast as they could! They were followed by the two policemen who were terrified. Both their hats had fallen off and the screaming dish was chasing them, hot on their heels!

Dam being diligent saw the danger and jumped out of the washing machine and picked up a stone and flung it at the dish. Luckily it clipped the side of it and it suddenly stopped and began to wobble and spin in the one place. It spun there screaming for a while until it slowed and the sound began to go down and down then it fell on its back and squashed Dam's be-you-tear-full daffodil patch!

The dish was dead. The terrified policemen laughed, they did not know what else to do! Dam offered them a cup of camomile tea to help calm them down!

7

Dam's Tyres

Once Dam was very poor because he dreamt there was oil beneath his house so he spent all his money on mining equipment the very next day.

Some months later he was in town looking in a shop window full of clothes.

He spied far away in a corner an old black fireman's coat with old brass buttons. Just what he needed!

It fitted perfectly and made him look like one thousand dollars. Dam forgot about his impoverishment and coughed up the money.

He put his coat on, puffed up his chest and opened the door to leave the shop. As the door opened a little bell rang like a fire-engine's bell and Dam paused a moment to look up at it before he went outside.

He jumped in his car with the shark skin leather seats and began on his merry way home. Dam secretly wanted to join the fire brigade so he mused that his blue car was red and had a flashing orange light on the top of it and soon he was sitting up, both hands on the wheel, making a very loud siren noise. Just as the noise became almost unbearable for his own ears there was an almighty explosion and the car shot off the road down an embankment and zig zagged in a whole lot of mud before coming to a halt behind some trees!

Dam thought he'd been shot and began to feel for holes! He seemed okay so he quickly opened the door and knelt beside the car. His ears were on high alert but he couldn't hear anybody - nothing! He was a long way from town. He looked for bullet holes in the side of his car, there were none. His heart sounded like a train!

Dam looked down and saw the problem. The car had a flat tyre!

"Oh no," he thought. "I can't afford to fix that!" He jacked the car up and studied the problem. Normal cars carry spare wheels but Dam's car was not normal.

"Damn!" said Dam as he realised it was one of those tyres without an inner tube. If he could drive it slowly home he could fix it there, he thought.

He looked around for a piece of rubber about ten metres long but there was only grass and trees.

He rummaged in the car and came out with rags everywhere, an old mosquito net, three pairs of socks and a few old apple cores!

He began to stuff these in the tyre. But that was not enough. Dam went back to the car where he found an old towel, a fan belt and another pair of socks.

But that was still not enough. Dam reluctantly began taking off the shark skin seat covers and with a stick he jammed those in the tyre as well. Still that was not enough!

"What an enormous space is in this tyre!" thought Dam. He took his shoes and socks off and jammed them in. Next he took his outside pants off, fortunately he had others on underneath! He reluctantly considered jamming his new fireman's coat in as well! However he decided against doing that as it was a cold day. Dam then stuffed his shirt in, but even that was not enough.

He suspected that the tyre was trying to swallow his coat as well but he was sure that was not going to happen!

He began to collect grass and leaves. They were difficult to squeeze into the crack so finally Dam took his coat off and began to look for his shirt in the wheel. Unfortunately the tyre seemed to have swallowed it up! He felt a chill wind as he began stuffing his brand new fireman's coat in the tyre, brass buttons and all.

"That will have to do," he said shivering as he began to screw up the wheel nuts and lower the car.

He was soon back in, trying to start the engine. Unfortunately a red light came on in the dash.

"Just like a fire engine!" he said under his breath.

The fan-belt had broken and the new-fan belt was in the tyre!

Dam jacked the car up again. He removed his coat which he put on again.

Then all the grass and leaves came out. Then his shirt which he put on under his coat. Next he found his pants and his shoes and socks. At least he was dressed again and not shivering, he thought. Next the shark skin seat covers came out, the mosquito net, rags everywhere and finally the fan belt wrapped up in a towel.

Dam put the new fan-belt in the car and the broken one in the tyre. Then he put the shark skin seat covers, his shoes and socks, grass and leaves, shirt, shoes, rags everywhere and pants back in the wheel as well as everything else. He took his coat off and plugged it all up with that. He started his car and went bumpity bump up onto the road.

By the time Dam arrived home he was blue with cold and the sun was nearly down. He jacked the car up but had to jack it down again as the wheel nuts had to be loosened when it was on the ground. He then jacked up the car again.

Dam removed the wheel and took it around the back to his work shed.

When he opened the tyre and tried to pull all his clothes out a horrible mess confronted him. For the whole lot had turned into a great big knot of indescribable complexity and it all came out at once. The tyre had half-digested his wardrobe!

It was all green! And if one looked carefully one noticed fabric, mud, apple cores and clothing all intertwined with mosquito net and rags everywhere.

His shoes were unrecognisable!

It was in the early hours of the morning when Dam finally untwined his coat. It was completely green and slimy and had severe creases all over it. Its arms had wrapped about itself in a tortured embrace. As he carefully unwound it he saw reflected in the candle light, the first glint of a brass button. At least the buttons had been beautifully cleaned he thought even though they had cut holes in the cloth. He held it up and examined it further. It had grass protruding from all over it as though he'd been fighting grass fires.

After he washed it the water was black and the coat was so heavy it nearly broke the clothes-line. He hung it up to dry which took a week and it still smelt like rubber and a grass fire!

He used it to go shopping in however he no longer felt like one thousand dollars, quite the opposite! He looked like an old fireman who had fought many fires. He was pleased its pockets were so large as people began giving him food.

It was sometime after the experience of the flat tyre when he had jammed his entire wardrobe in the tyre that Dam decided to buy a spare wheel for his car. To save money he went to a car-wrecker and found an old one that fitted perfectly!

There at the wreckers was a car just like his own so he bought one of its wheels. Because the wheel was still on the car Dam offered to take it off.

He loosened the nuts and jacked up the car but soon jacked it down again as he realised he was on the wrong side of the car and that particular tyre was worn a little. He did up the nuts again. He jacked up the car on the other side but soon jacked it down again as he'd forgotten to loosen the nuts. He loosened the nuts and jacked up the car. One of the nuts was still tight so he had to jack the car down again to undo it properly. He then jacked up the car and took off the wheel.

Dam jacked up his own car after loosening the wheel nuts though one of them was still tight so he jacked the car down again to loosen it. Then he jacked it up and took the wheel off. He put his new wheel on. Just as he was doing the first nut up the car took a sudden unexpected leap forward, gripped the jack by its extension bar and came crashing to the ground. The jack was jammed underneath the car.

Dam had to borrow another jack from the wrecker so he could jack his car up again which he did. His old jack was tightly jammed and needed to be belted with a large hammer before it came loose.

Eventually out it came so Dam jacked up the car a little more. He put on the wheel and did the nuts up. Then he jacked the car down and tightened the nuts. Dam jumped in and drove off with his new wheel.

Some distance along the road at the top of a busy bridge a car the same as his was in the middle of the road! It had broken down. A little old lady was in it wondering what to do. Dam pulled over and went back to see what the problem was. The lady was frightened as big trucks and busses were flashing past.

Dam peeped in the window and straightened his back. The car had not one but two flat tyres!

"Hang on," said Dam racing to his car. He struggled back with the jack and his old tyre. "I can fix it!" he said.

Dam was just able to push the car half into the breakdown lane and half out. It was too much for him to get it any further. He jacked up the car with trucks and busses flying past but soon jacked it down again. He undid the wheel nuts and jacked the car up again. One of the nuts was too tight so he jacked the car down, loosened the nut and then jacked the car up again. Every time a car or truck passed the car wobbled precariously on the jack.

As he put the wheel on he only did up three nuts hand tight. Dam jacked the car down and went to the other side of the car re-arranging the blocks and various shoes he had used as wedges to stop the car rolling. Dam jacked up the car but soon jacked it down again. Now he said,

"Damn!" as Dam was dithering and Dam doesn't get mad at much let alone Dam! He looked at himself in the hubcap. He was getting used to the image of his extended jaw, giant nose and huge lips, with the little beady eyes way above watching. He stuck his green tongue out.

"Blithering idiot!" he said to himself.

He undid the nuts and jacked up the car again. He took off the wheel and put his spare on. He did the nuts up hand tight then jacked the car down again where he did them up fully. When he looked at the other wheel it had moved slightly from its place so he jacked the car up again on that side and put the extra nuts on hand tight. He finally jacked the car down for the last time and tightened the nuts but forgot to remove the jack from the side of the car and put it back in his boot.

The woman was so pleased and took down Dam's phone number so she could return his wheel.

"Dam Jelly Arms!" thought Dam, was a good surname for himself as he got back in his car.

As he was driving down the slight hill to his house he noticed a wheel flying ahead of him down the road!

"Hey!" he cried, "Somebody's lost a wheel!" Then his steering wheel wrenched itself sideways and the front of his car fell on the road and dribbled to a halt!

Dam leapt out and chased the wheel past his house. On and on it rolled and stopped finally at the bottom of the hill. He pushed it back up and went to his boot to look for the jack. Much to his dismay he couldn't find it. Then he realised he'd left it sticking out the side of the ladies car!

Dam was considerably jacked about that and he remembered his face in the hubcap.

8

Dam and the Washing Machine

Dam woke up. He was wet and moving quickly. There was a great roaring sound in his ears, then something grabbed him and pulled him under. He held his breath but water ran up his nose. Desperately he grabbed something solid and reefed himself up. He broke through the surface and could see daylight. Something had him by the neck again and was dragging him under. He stood up but lost his balance. Now he knew where he was, he'd fallen in the washing machine.

He made a desperate grasp for the edge of it but it was too slippery and down he went again. The clothes were upon him like one thousand tentacles all clutching to drag him down. With a great effort he hauled himself out but found his feet were tangled. He made a jab for the stop switch as he went around, he jabbed again, missed, jabbed again, missed. Then he noticed the electric lead sitting humbly in the power point. He lunged for it and caught it by the tail as it were and pulled it out of the wall.

He was so giddy the room kept spinning round and round for ages.

He slumped onto the side of the monster and blew bubbles of dark water out of his nose. His eyes were stinging. He launched a leg over the side with a few straggling socks attached and hung there a while as his other foot was still entangled. He reached in and parted the dark water to find his foot. He found a shoe but it was vacant of foot. So he pulled his leg a little harder. Out it came clothes and all. The floor looked like monsters entrails wet with dark blood.

Dam heaved it all back in and set the wash-cycle he must have been dreaming. He simply couldn't remember what he'd been doing before he started the washing. He was sure he didn't go to sleep in the washing machine or had he?

Dam went and had some breakfast. He made sure to take his pills beforehand as they were designed to make him less forgetful. After all he was one hundred and three and getting on a bit. He could remember his childhood clearly but things that happened yesterday or even an hour ago were easily forgotten.

He swallowed twenty pills and went to clean his teeth. He had one of those new tooth brushes which bent in the middle so you could clean your tonsils as well! It even revved and sang a deep song to you. He used to have an electric one but that got caught in something down his throat and he had to gargle, as he could not talk, to the nurse in Casually (Casualty) at the Horse-piddle (Hospital). She was such a slow person he remembered. She asked Dam what was wrong!

Dam looked in the mirror. It was a very small one, about the size of one eyeball. He had a larger one but he spent so much time talking to it he had to put it outside. He looked at a single eye.

"Typically bloodshot" he said and pulled down the bottom lid. "Sick!" he said to himself as his nose came monstrously into view before his next eye lined up. "Must have some chronic disease" he whispered as he began to walk around the house.

Dam had taken up doing exercise lately since he'd been taking the pills.

His favourite thing to do was to walk around the house. Any further afield and he might get lost or fall off a cliff or bump into a tree. This way if he hit another window like he did the other week, he could crawl inside and bandage the wound, like he did the other week.

He walked carefully looking out for open windows. There were none. At least he had learnt to keep them all closed. After sometime he began to feel quite weary so he staggered inside and fell into a couch. After a while he turned around and sat in it properly. He was soon fast asleep. Sometime later he woke up. It was dark. His tummy was empty and he felt hungry. He picked himself up and went into the kitchen. He made sure before he had more food to have some more pills.

"Sick," he said as he scoffed them down. The pills were awfully huge and quite pretty with blue and pink speckles all over them. He took one into the bathroom and held it up to the mirror. It was as large as his eyeball and almost the same colour. He went back to stir some foul black concoction he'd emptied out of a few packets marked 'Health Food, Vitamin and Mineral Supplement.'

"This'll fix me!" he said as he gulped it down.

Poor Dam was violently ill and vomited all over his favourite clock above the sink. Half-digested tablets and black stuff sprayed all over the wall. He gasped and crawled into bed!

Sometime later he woke up. It was dark so he went back to sleep. He woke up again and it was still dark, so he went back to sleep. When he woke up for the third time he felt a little better. It was just getting light or was it? No it was growing dark. So he went back to sleep. When he woke up again in the dark and wondered how long had he slept for.

He sat up in bed and read a magazine however the light was too bright and the words hurt his eyes. He needed a drink of water so he climbed out of bed and fell over. The floor was spinning round and round. His bed seemed to have wings. He staggered into the toilet and apart from some incredibly loud explosions nothing happened!

He crawled into the kitchen and heaved himself up to the level of the sink. There he found piles of washing up and somebody had thrown food all over the wall and the clock! It never kept the right time anyway and if it was right it was indecipherable. It was making a noise but its hands were stuck.

Dam found his nose in the mirror but his eyes were hard to find. He found one but not the other. He was sure he had another eye somewhere, he felt his face. Suddenly something appeared in the mirror which frightened him, it was vivid green. It took him a while to work out that it was his tongue.

He shuffled back to his bedroom through the piles of clothes. He lent on the door handle which was a tap. Some idiot had put a tap on the door! Dam didn't think it was funny. He lowered himself onto the bed and his little knobbly knees creaked like old door hinges. He flung himself beyond his dreams, back to sleep.

Dam was wakened by a tap on the door. The birds were calling so he figured it was morning. He crawled out of bed and manoeuvred towards the front door. There were people on his doorstep dressed in bank clothes! Dam opened the door.

"Good morning sir, it's a lovely day!" Dam looked them up and down.

They were selling something. "We were just wondering if you….er…. were happy with your situation for we'd like to give you some information on the Good Lord." They handed Dam a small magazine. Dam didn't say much, he managed to blurt out,

"Time fine, wank you." Whether it was the warm sun or the look on Dam's bedraggled face which made the group turn and walk away Dam didn't know. He shut his mouth but found to his surprise that his tongue was hanging out.

He took the magazine back to bed, it had a picture of a little girl with a baby lamb under an orange tree on the front. Dam looked at the pile of magazines next to his bed and read the covers 'Mr Universe 1889,' 'The Ultimate Muscle,' 'Mr Universe 2003.' Somehow, Dam wondered, ever since he'd been doing muscle building and minding his health, he'd been feeling off colour.

He looked at the weights in the corner of his room. He'd made them out of car tyres filled with cement. Even the thought of lifting them made him feel exhausted.

He lay down and opened the little magazine. It read, "The Lord has the biggest muscles in the universe, and the biggest heart." Dam had never heard of this guy before, his followers looked very scrawny.

Dam floated out to the kitchen. He'd run out of one bottle of pills, only five left. He drank them down with some orange juice he'd bought at the supermarket in a cardboard container. It was old and fizzed into the glass.

He tipped the rest down the sink.

He looked out the window at his own orange tree and saw that it was laden with fruit. Desperately he struggled outside through the window - his legs were in control. He hobbled quickly over to it through the jungle of grass. His back felt as stiff as cardboard as he reached up to pick some fruit. Sometime after, back inside after eating them, he looked up at the clock, it was still working.

Sometimes Dam wished he ran on batteries and never broke down or stopped like the clock. He didn't care about his dreams they were long dead.

His stomach began to make weird noises, maybe the oranges were poisonous?

"No, no," he said to himself, "Oranges are real!" Dam went over to the sink and washed a few dishes, he began to clean up. He actually began to feel a whole lot better, even hungry. He looked in the fridge for something to eat and found a whole lot of food in cardboard packages. He opened one which read rice and vegetables. He emptied it into a saucepan. It looked like fish food.

He looked out the window at the orange tree and several moments later found himself sitting under the tree eating oranges again.

"I wonder if the Lord eats oranges?" he said.

All of a sudden Dam had an enormous burst of energy! He became so energised he didn't know what to do! He ran back inside and dived upon his weights. He found he could lift them time and time again even with one arm! He ran to the mirror and easily found an eye. What was wrong with him?

The energy was most unusual. He opened some windows and smelt the fresh air then he went into the kitchen and began to mop the floor! He even mopped the walls and the clock!

"How come the clock never gets tired?" he wondered. Dam began to pick up all the clothes about the house and throw them in the laundry.

There was something about the laundry he was unsure of. As though there was a dark force in there which was tempting him in. He didn't like the laundry, not now at least, so he shut the door.

He went outside and sniffed the air. The day was bright and sunny. He began to jog around the house. He hadn't moved so fast in years!

Bang! He slammed into a window. It flung him backwards onto the ground. He felt his forehead and a large lump was already forming. He staggered inside holding one eye. Cautiously he approached the mirror and could just make out a large lump above a rapidly swelling eye. He went to the fridge and filled a bandage up with a whole lot of frozen peas. He wrapped them around his forehead and his eye.

Apart from his black eye he felt fine. He went back outside.

"Oranges away!" he yelled in defiance and gently shut the window. He began walking and kept one eye out for windows. As he walked around his house with great strides he felt the muscles of his legs.

"Good Lord!" he said as he remembered the lamb and the little girl under the orange tree.

Sometime passed and Dam began to realise he was unstoppable. He wasn't getting tired. On his way past the kitchen window he looked in at the clock. "I'm better than you!" he said.

As night fell Dam's walk began to slow, until the last circumnavigation of his house brought him exhausted to the other tap he'd fixed to the front door.

He staggered inside and sat down in the kitchen. His knees creaked as the chair took his puny frame.

"Argh!" he said bending his legs. He hobbled over to the fridge and was just about to open the door when he noticed his vitamin and mineral supplements on the shelf.

"Oh no wonder I'm tired!" He said as he reached up and took them down.

He made a large bowel of pumpkin soup and emptied the packet of supplements into it and stirred until it turned black. He undid his bandage and added the peas.

"This'll fix me up!" he said as he wolfed it all down. It tasted ghastly.

Dam sat bolt upright.

"The washing!" he exclaimed out loud. He raced into the laundry and opened the washing machine. His mouldy wet clothes had congealed together.

They came out in a solid furry, smelly mass. He threw them back in and heaped some more clothes on top of them then put several scoops of 'Mother's All' washing powder in and set the wash cycle.

"If I hadn't had my vitamins I would never have remembered these clothes," he said. He added more soap powder and watched it going round forming clouds of bubbles and landscapes.

Dam woke up suddenly. He was wet and moving quickly. There was a great roaring sound in his ears, and then something grabbed him and pulled him under. He stood up but lost his balance. Now he knew where he was, he'd fallen in the washing machine.

9

Dam and the Tractor

Dam loved cars but he loved tractors more. He liked working on cars partly because he found it so difficult. It was really the challenge of getting it right which enticed him. He remembered the first time he changed the oil. After he'd put the new oil in he found a large oil puddle spreading rapidly out on the ground around the front of the car! He could do nothing as it soaked quickly into the ground. That wasn't the first; it was the second time he'd forgotten to reinstall the oil drain bolt in the bottom of the motor. Dam always seemed to do things in twos or threes, before he got it right.

He could do most things, however he didn't like fixing steering problems because he knew he'd run into the only tree in his paddock if he did, so he left the steering for other people to do. He worked on the brakes and checked everything three times just to make sure he could stop if it looked like he was about to crash into the tree. He had accidentally flattened all the others!

Dam had learnt how to work on tractors because he'd worked on cars.

Now in his one hundredth year he knew a little about how they worked.

One day Dam was driving along in his great big orange tractor when he accidentally crashed into the very last tree in the paddock. He climbed down and surveyed the damage. There was a lot of bark missing but the tree would survive. However the tractor had a bent front axle and Dam scratched his head and tried to think how he could fix it.

He went to his shed and came back with a strong rope. He thought he could tie the rope to the tree then around his axle and bend it back in to shape. He tied it all up and revved the engine.

Well it certainly bent the axle but not the right one as the tree fell across the back of the tractor and bent the rear axle, narrowly missing Dam! He was lucky to be alive.

Now he had two bent axles! Fortunately he could still start the old engine by connecting the solenoid to the battery as the ignition key didn't work. Eventually he made a meandering path back up to his house on the hill.

There was no way he could fix the axles himself so he rang the tractor repair place in town and prepared to drive it in to be fixed. Dam's tractor was quite large and at the best of times it was difficult to steer. It was like a huge orange dragon and had a voice like a thousand drums.

He drove past the school at 3:00 o'clock when everybody was leaving and all the children gazed in wonder at the giant machine which drove erratically down the road. Dam gave three waves and all the children waved back three times.

The road went around a small dam then up a hill to the garage. He struggled with the steering as he went around the dam. He was lucky he didn't drive into it! Then up the hill to the tractor repair shed. When he arrived his arms were worn out from trying to control the heavy machine.

He climbed down and was standing at the back of the tractor talking to the man when there was a very loud pop and violent hissing as water suddenly sprayed from the back wheel all over both of them! Not from one hole but two! The tractor had a flat tyre!

For those of you who do not know about tractors they have water in their wheels to help them stay upright on steep slopes. Dam said damn as water dribbled off his nose which began to smell of old rubber.

"You'll have to fix that too," he said to the man. Dam rode his bicycle home wondering how much it was all going to cost. He went into the garden and picked beans for his dinner. He didn't like other people fixing his machines because he liked to learn how to fix them himself. He enjoyed finding out how things worked.

That night he dreamed he was surrounded by large orange tractors all in bits and pieces. Each piece had a face on it and when Dam picked them up and placed them where they needed to go, the faces smiled. Dam climbed onto one tractor but it would not start.

The next day he woke early, it was going to be a hot day. When the sun was high in the sky at about midday, he sniffed the air.

"Bushfire!" he said and sniffed again.

Sure enough in the direction of the town, a fire had sprung up. There was a strong wind as well. Dam watched as the brown and black smoke billowed into the sky. He heard fire engines and strange explosions. He looked again and realised it was very close to the tractor repair shed.

"Oh my tractor, I hope it's alright!" he said.

He was turning to go inside when the phone rang. It was the tractor repair man in a very agitated state.

"I can't start your tractor and there's a huge fire coming this way!" Dam put the phone down, he ran to his bicycle and charged down to the road. His legs had never gone so fast. He flew past his bean field and said he should use his legs to plough the earth. Then he charged past the school where all the children were gathered outside waiting for the fire engine. They all saw Dam flash past and all their heads moved at once. Dam slowed on the hill but when he saw that the tractor shed was on fire his legs became like real pistons in an engine!

The repair man was there jumping about with a tiny hose and hardly any water.

"I fixed the wheel but I couldn't start it!" he yelled.

The fire had engulfed the shed and to Dam's horror his tractor's back wheels were on fire! Black smoke filled the shed so Dam crouched low and ran over to his machine. He climbed underneath and fuzzed the solenoid to the battery.

A great roar like a thousand drums sounded amongst the flames as the tractor started. Dam climbed aboard his huge machine.

"Wooah!" he said as the tractor reared up on its back wheels and charged out of the shed. He revved the engine as though the earth was on fire and charged down the hill with flames and black smoke billowing out from behind. He was heading straight for the dam but the damn thing wouldn't steer! It went one way and then the other!

The startled children looked and saw the flaming tractor come roaring out of the shed and come hurtling towards them, out of control! It went towards the dam then the school, then the dam again – then,

"Bang! Crash!" it broke through the school gate and suddenly stopped in the middle of the playground. Dam had finally found the brake! He jumped off wide eyed and a little singed as he ran towards the road. He turned to watch his tractor burning. Then unexpectedly the two back wheels exploded and water showered everywhere! Meanwhile the fire had reached one of the other classrooms. It was burning fiercely when the fire engine arrived and luckily put it out.

Dam's eyes began to feel sore. Was it because of the smoke or was it because they were beginning to weep diesel! His tractor was a burnt out mess!

However he was very pleased that it had saved part of the school! All the children were safe of course. The newspapers called Dam a courageous man who had saved the school from fire.

"Don't worry" said the tractor repair man, "I'm insured, you'll get a completely new tractor." Dam went home on his bicycle. Life was suddenly lonely without a tractor.

Several weeks later Dam drove home on his brand new orange tractor. It had new paint, new oil, new grease, it would last a lifetime. All the children came out of the school to have a look and Dam waved three times. The children waved three times back and Dam waved back twice.

He used the tractor to plough up his paddock ready to plant beans. He even used it to stand his only tree back up in the field.

"What would I do without a tractor?" he said as he looked at all the pictures the children had drawn for him of his big orange tractor saving the school.

He went outside to admire it; each angle, each nut and bolt. He decided to check the oil.

There was none! He looked under the engine and found that the oil drain bolt was missing!

10

Dam Builds a Helicopter

Dam lived on the edge of the forest next to a tall black mountain.

Aeroplanes had crashed into the forest on the mountain because it was so high and it often generated dangerous storms. Dam would look up and watch the lightning strike the tall cliffs and illuminate the trees as they thrashed about in the wind.

Dam wasn't afraid of lightning so long as he had shoes on. He had been struck several times and apart from being temporally blinded it made him feel quite good; in fact it had cured his cold. For some reason, Dam didn't know why lightning liked him and seemed to be attracted to him especially when he didn't have shoes on. Dam was sure that when he wore shoes the lightning went away. Another odd thing he noticed after being struck was that it made his hair stand on end, turned it purple and made it grow very rapidly. He didn't like his hair that colour so generally he wore shoes when storms were about.

One day he watched a helicopter hovering around the cliffs and straight away he decided to build a flying machine to look at the cliffs himself. Not a large one with an engine in it, just a small one which would lift him up and down gently.

He set to work designing and then building his contraption. He bought a whole lot of flat boards to make the propeller with. Basically the helicopter was a great big propeller and nothing more. Dam was planning on suspending himself underneath it and hoped it would lift him into the sky.

He set about carving the blades of the six metre diameter propeller blades with great care and skill. Each was fixed into a central hub made out of soft wood and strengthened with wire and glue. He put two holes in the bottom of the hub for two lugs which came up from a wheel below it. This wheel had a large hole in its centre through which a swivelling basket was suspended and attached to the centre of the propeller above.

His idea was to mount this contraption on a launching platform in his back yard and coil a long rope around the wheel which was more like a barrel with a space in its centre. One end of the rope would be tied to a very springy tree, the other end he intended to wrap around the barrel with the lugs in its top.

The rope would not be tied to the barrel and the barrel would spin on strong ball bearings at its base. Dam found a special long springy tree which he cut down and dragged back to the launching site with his tractor.

He spent ages mounting both the propeller and the tree horizontally at just the right height. He bent the tree back with his tractor and made a short trigger rope which he planned to cut with an axe to release the tree and set the barrel spinning. He mounted the propeller on the lugs at the top of the barrel.

Dam hoped to pop out of this barrel in his swivelling basket and fly up into the air.

He planned to steer himself once airborne, by pointing in the direction he wanted to go with one arm while batting a kind-of large fly swat with the other. The weight of his arm pointing on one side of the basket would hopefully tip the balance and guide him.

All was ready. Dam needed a very calm windless day with no storms.

The day he chose for the launch turned out to be a bad one and no sooner had he started the engine of his tractor than clouds began to form on the mountain and the thunder rumbled. Dam went up to his house and sat on his veranda with shoes on. From there he watched the lightning dancing about the cliffs deep into the night.

Some local people used to see fire-balls and strange lights, some even believed that flying saucers came out of a large hole in the cliffs at night.

Dam kept watching the mountain, he'd always wanted to get closer to it for all those strange stories had made him more curious and he wanted to explore.

Next day was perfect, the sun was out and it was quiet and peaceful with no wind.

He dressed for his first flight in bright yellow just in case he became lost.

He didn't bother doing a test flight he knew it would all work. He started his tractor, bent the tree back and tied it tight with the trigger rope. Then he coiled the other rope tightly around the big wheel below the propeller. Everything was set so he climbed into his little hanging basket. His heart began to pound as he looked up at the mountain and said,

"Here I come!" He reached out with one arm and cut the trigger rope.

Barely had Dam dropt the axe when a great whirring noise came from the propeller as the tree sprung back powerfully. He hung on as the air rushed around and all of a sudden with a great whoosh he was airborne! The ground below him quickly disappeared.

He was propelled so high his house looked like a tiny speck. After a while he gained some control of his fear of heights and began to point furiously at the mountain and wave his fly-swat. He began to descend towards the cliffs, slowly at first and then faster and faster. His helicopter worked better than he'd dreamed though it was somewhat uncontrollable.

As he flew near the cliffs he noticed they were much rougher than he expected with crevasses, trees and caves. Then a terrible thing happened, a breeze off the mountain caught the propeller and sent it headlong into a large tree which was hanging out of the cliff. Fortunately he landed quite lightly in it and looked down. His house was hundreds of meters below him and the tree was impossible to climb. He was stuck. The propeller was well and truly jammed in the branches. Somehow he was going to have to climb down and find a way up the cliff. The breeze was ruffling his hair as he prepared to climb down. But the trunk was too large and he couldn't put his arms around it.

He would have to stay there like a large yellow bird and hope that someone would see him and come to his rescue.

Little did he realise that that is exactly what was going on back in the real world. Many people sent reports to the local newspapers saying they'd seen an unidentified flying object disappear into a large cave in the cliffs. The reports said the object was huge and moved at incredible speed, describing it as suddenly stopping and rapidly changing direction before whisking off silently. The air force had been informed and the news spread rapidly.

Meanwhile Dam sat in a fork of the tree like a large yellow koala bear.

He was so pleased his helicopter worked. Already he was considering his next flight.

Gradually the wind became stronger and clouds appeared, swirling above him and in no time he was surrounded by the cold wet air of dense cloud.

He lost sight of the cliff and could barely see the propeller above him.

The daylight faded and night came down like a deep black sea.

"Oh no!" he said to himself as a storm began to grow and the leaves in the tree began to blow this way and that. The wind dislodged the propeller and sent it crashing into the cliff before it fell into the black forest below.

And then the thunder roared. Already Dam's hair was standing on end. It was going to be a long night. The whole mountain was groaning and calling out to Dam, he began to shiver as much from cold as from fear.

A fine rain began to sting his face and then heavy drops bounced off the tree trunk in front of him. Occasionally the clouds would clear and when the lightning flickered he could see the huge black dripping face of the craggy cliffs in front of him while on the other side was the warmth of his house beyond the black abyss. As the lightning flashed nearer and nearer he could see the shapes of the trees on the cliff top writhing and thrashing their limbs with the torment of the wind.

Then a loud crackle, sizzle and a blinding flash and instantly a loud crash of thunder and Dam had been struck by a million volts! The soles of his shoes were blown off, his hair was definitely standing on end and his toes began to tingle. For some time great showers of shooting multi-coloured sparks danced off the cliff face and fizzed about him, some stuck in his hair! He hung on to his tree for dear life as spears of lightning shot out of the cliff-face and kept striking him.

Dam began to feel quite warm. He felt his hair and it seemed to have grown twenty centimetres and in the flashes of lightning he could see that his hair was turning purple again.

He didn't get much sleep that night the lightning would not leave him alone. Like a bad dream it hovered about him striking him when he least expected it.

After what seemed a lifetime the first glimmers of the early dawn flittered across the face of the old dark cliff.

The storm had gone. Dam stretched and yawned. His hair was a meter long and bright purple! The cloud had lifted and a blue day was about to begin.

He lay across a limb with his hair hanging down and his arms and legs dangling either side of the trunk, he closed his eyes and was soon fast asleep.

Dam woke up with a great start there was thunder in his ears and a wind in his hair. Right beside him was a huge helicopter hovering. He waved and squealed,

"Help!" though he knew they would not hear him.

Dam could see the people in the helicopter taking photographs of him.

Little did he realise they thought he was an alien. He thought he was going to be rescued but the helicopter disappeared and he was left alone again. His tummy rumbled so he ate some leaves.

Back at base the photographs were developed and examined carefully by military and aviation experts. 'Alien Visits Earth!' the pictures were splashed all over the newspapers and television, both here and overseas. Some stories which appeared in the papers described a 'yellow and purple monster' which was unable to get back into its hole in the cliff. Others said it was brought down by the storm and had come from a distant galaxy!

Luckily for Dam his neighbour who was a little old lady recognised him from the newspaper clippings. To make sure she went next door to see if he was at home. There she found the odd looking launching pad, the tractor and the springy tree. She rang the newspaper.

"That's not an alien, that's my neighbour Mr Diligent!" News spread fast. Dam had spent another night alone in his tree and once again the lightning had tickled his toes. His hair was two meters long and his ears were going bright green. He had eaten so many gum leaves he had begun to grow hair on the backs of his hands.

Dam could be seen from the ground now. It looked like the tree was full of purple blossom. People began gathering at vantage points to view the tree- climbing creature from outer space.

"He's incredibly ugly!" said one person with binoculars.

"Looks really dangerous!" said another.

"I think we should shoot and ask questions later!" somebody said.

That morning the army helicopter roared up the mountain again. It hovered above Dam's tree and a man was lowered down on a wire cable.

"Oh!" said Dam, "Am I ever pleased to see you!"

They took him back to base and gave him a cup of tea but the tea began to boil in the cup as he put it to his lips. They gave him a pair of scissors which Dam cut his hair with as sparks flew all about him threatening to catch fire.

Finally he looked normal. The commander came in and shook his hand.

But Dam was highly charged with electricity and burnt the commander's hand so badly sparks came out of his ears and his hair stood on end! Dam apologised profusely and was taken to horse-piddle (hospital) but they didn't know what to do. They put a voltmeter in his mouth like a thermometer and it melted. He was given an electric light to hold and it exploded. Dam was supercharged!

They took him to the power station and did more tests. They found out he could charge batteries by simply touching them and for a long while he was kept busy charging batteries as they tried to flatten him and get rid of some of his energy. He sat in a room all alone holding two large electric wires. Nothing seemed to work he was thoroughly electrified.

Eventually he collected his bundle of purple hair, thanked the people for rescuing him and went home.

Dam's life had changed somewhat. To cook a meal all he had to do was put a finger in the pot and the water would boil. Talking to him was dangerous as sparks flashed between his teeth when he opened his mouth and his voice had a crackly ring to it. He felt quite well though and from day to day went about his business as usual, occasionally looking up at the mountain and the tree which had claimed his helicopter.

He'd taken a liking to gum leaves and had made a rug out of his purple hair. He wasn't afraid of lightning anymore, on the contrary he began to feel off colour if he didn't have his once a month lightning strike and quite often during storms one could find him out in the open with lightning dancing all around him. On these occasions he would often start singing and it wasn't long before the little old lady from next-door rang him up and offered him a job.

"Would you like to sing in my band?" she asked. The lady had connections with rock and roll bands overseas. Dam's knees began to feel electric like he was eighteen years old! He went for an audition at her place and cracked all the mirrors in the house as well as two windows!

"You're hired" they had told him.

To cut a long story short, he became a famous rock and roll star. They called him Rocket Legs. His voice was coarse grained and so loud one had to wear ear-muffs ten meters away.

His debut night on tour was an outdoor concert, one warm and humid evening in America. As he was about to go on stage the first clap of thunder exploded over the crowd. And then his first note was accompanied by an ear splitting sizzle and another huge clap of thunder.

He suddenly became a huge hit and glowed electric blue for ten seconds!

Then his voice was so loud people covered their ears and then their eyes as the lightning illuminated him like a giant multi-coloured spark. Blue flames shot out of his head and many people dropped silently to their knees.

Unfortunately his manager found him to be a liability and his carrier ended that night. They found his electrifying act on stage was far too dangerous.

This particular night there had been a complete blackout of the concert except for Dam on stage who lit up the whole field! He looked like a giant fire-fly on stage with the jitters. Three people had heart attacks and many had to be sent to horse-piddle (hospital) suffering shock.

Back home sometime later Dam set up a small business selling purple rugs. He had learnt all he wanted to know about the mountain having explored it in a flying machine. He decided to leave the mountain alone preferring instead to let the mountain come to him.

11

Dam Goes Pod Fishing

Dam woke up one morning and sniffed the air. He was like that, a veritable hound. He sniffed before he talked, sniffed mail before he opened it and sniffed his food and his tooth brush before cleaning his teeth. It was his sixth sense and he used it to its full extent. He had to, ever since some kind of cricket had built its nest inside one of his nostrils and gone to sleep in there and woken Dam up because it started snoring loudly.

He cleared his nose by sniffing and a whole lot of mud went down into his lungs and the cricket latched onto something down inside his throat which swelled up and prevented him from breathing. Dam had to quickly jam his bicycle pump down his throat and pump it as he drove along to the horse-piddle (hospital). A police officer pulled him over because he thought Dam was waving at him.

Dam at times had found other strange creatures in his nose such as a large hairy caterpillar, a number of blow-flies and a wasp. Insects obviously had a fascination for it.

"Inconveniently large" he admitted.

He had used it once in a brass street band. He modified it with various inserts and it became a peculiar kind of wind instrument. He had a particular solo part in the chorus which they allotted to his playing. That career stopped abruptly one afternoon when he lost his way while playing for he could not see where he was going because his hands kept fiddling in front of his cross-eyed face in order to make the sound. Which meant that he could not see out nor could anybody see in.

Consequently Dam was very fond of sniffing. This particular morning the air came to him as fresh and sweet as a rising tide...

"Fishing!" he exclaimed.

"Today I'm going fishing!" He was delighted to see the tea leaves in the bottom of his tea cup form into the shape of a fish. He sniffed the cup.

"This is surely a sign that I'll catch a big fish!"

Years ago Dam had been a keen fisherman and loved the sea most dearly. Now that he'd moved to the country he could still smell it in his veins especially when the tide was in. When he lived near the sea he found it monopolised his life so much that he had to watch its every mood to make sure he didn't miss anything special. He spent hours staring at it, or swimming in it, or fishing.

There was more than salt in his veins there was seaweed, shells, plankton and jellyfish. He was a walking marine reserve!

Not far from where he lived was a long beach which was fished often by enthusiastic pod fishermen. Since the tide came in a long way these fishermen would hire a tall tripod which they called a "pod." They would place it in a special spot at low tide and sit in a special seat on top and fish the high tide as the water swirled about them. It wasn't dangerous so long as one chose the right spot to place the pod.

Dam rumbled under the house sniffing and found his old fishing basket.

It was covered in cobwebs. When he opened it he found an old dried lunch he'd forgotten to eat years ago or was it bait? In amongst the tangle of line he came across a small round container full of hooks and to Dam's delight they were only slightly rusty. At the bottom of the basket he found his old crumpled fishing hat. It had a few feathered fly lures in it left over from when he went trout fishing. He dusted it, sniffed and coughed and put it on his head. He loved this hat. It was given to him by a special friend.

"I'll take my fly rod as well," he said.

It was a good day for fishing, the sky was overcast and there was no wind. Dam spent an hour cleaning and preparing all his lines. He sharpened the hooks until they glistened, as sharp as a bee sting. He then made a small lunch of four bacon and banana sandwiches, two eggs, one large slice of fruit cake and a bottle of strawberry jam and half a lettuce.

He grabbed his special fly rod and the long handled landing net and bounded down the garden path to his faithful little car. Dam usually took the car fishing for it had a propeller at the back of it. He would wind down the window and turn the radio on and leave the line out until the news came on then he'd wind the line in and catch the news. Somehow fishing had become incredibly boring without the news. This time Dam was going to fish in a different way.

Pod fishing, he hoped it would be more exciting.

He arrived at the bait and tackle shop where he intended to hire his pod.

They had all sorts of shapes and sizes some were quite luxurious with park benches on the tops of them. It was like looking at the Eiffel tower! Dam chose a medium size one with a small seat.

The person in the shop recommended mullies for bait. Dam looked down at them squirming about in the smelly sawdust bowl.

"They're maggots!" he said sniffing.

"No mullies," said the man, "You keep them alive by putting them under your bottom lip. They're perfectly clean," he added.

Dam bought forty of them and kept them in a little bag. He picked up the great steel ladder-pod-structure and lumbered down onto the sand. The tide was low and the sea was four hundred meters away. Dam struggled as best he could sniffing the sand and huffing and puffing. Other pod fishermen were taking up their positions and Dam kept some distance away from them.

In the muddy sand he could see the evidence of crabs and snails beneath the surface; they made lines and bumps here and there between the straggly bits of weed.

Dam set up the pod and climbed up. He looked out to sea and waited for the tide to change. After a little while he realised the tide was not yet out. So he climbed down, picked up the pod and walked further towards the sea. When he reached the small waves he decided to keep walking so he carried the pod out into the small surf until the water was up to his knees.

He climbed up his tower and watched as the tide began to turn. He looked around and could see other pod fishermen who must have looked as silly as he, sitting way up high above the waves.

All of a sudden the pod began to sink sideways in the sand. Dam scrambled to the highest side and began to jump up and down. That only made the contraption sink deeper. He looked at the sea and wondered if he'd be alright and not get swept off.

It was too late to move it he decided as the waves grew larger and the water deeper. Dam sat lopsided on his pod. It felt like it might topple over at any moment. At least there was a place to put the basket and a sort of a spot for one's feet. He folded his arms sniffed the air and like an eagle kept an eye out for fish. Some distance off he could see some birds gathering and beyond them was a large sea eagle. Dam felt sure he would catch something.

After some time of sitting sideways Dam's bottom grew very sore. There was still some time to wait before the tide was fully in so he took his hat off and sat on that.

"Yeow!" he cried as he shot into the air. His hat had fish hooks in it and Dam had one stuck in his bottom! With a great effort he swivelled around nearly losing his balance and tried to see what had speared him. His hat was quite firmly stapled to his bottom and the only way free was to cut the hook out of the hat. Dam got his razor sharp fishing knife out of his basket and began to cut a hole in his special hat. After some time it was free so he put it back on his head. Next he cut a hole in his pants and pulled the end of the hook through the hole.

Dam looked around; he was going to have to remove his pants to see how the hook was fixed. He didn't like the idea of doing that so he tried to twist his bottom sideways to have a look. It was no good the fly-lure was deeply imbedded, its little feathers blowing in the slight breeze. Dam said damn as he slid his pants down to his knees. He kept pulling on the hook and giving little whimpers of pain! It was no good. He tried making little cuts beside it but the hook was in fast. With great displeasure he pulled his pants back up and realised he'd have to stand.

The tide had advanced considerably and Dam set his mind back on fishing. Just below him he noticed a few small fish swimming around the legs of the pod.

"Ah," he said "I'll catch some of them for bait." He opened the mullie bag and was disappointed to see that they were barely moving.

"They're dying!" he said as he poked one with his finger. He took it out and looked at it. They had little frills along one edge and no mouth or head that Dam could see. They didn't really look like maggots after all.

Dam put one under his bottom lip. It lay there and didn't move. He took a small line out of his bag and was just about to sit down when he remembered the hook in his bottom. He found a small line and a small hook. He put the hook in his mouth so he wouldn't drop it and found the end of the line. He tied the hook on the line and was about to put a mullie on it from his mouth when a terrible thing happened. The whole basket slid off the platform and landed in the water.

"Oh no!" cried Dam as he leapt down the ladder. He quickly grabbed the landing net and after a little difficulty managed to hook it onto a part of the open lid. Fortunately it had landed the right way up and Dam retrieved it completely intact though he wondered about his lunch and the bait. Every time he moved his pants rubbed against the hook so he carefully scrambled back up to the platform. Suddenly this whole process of pod fishing became ridiculous to Dam and just as he was about to reach the top of the ladder a sharp pain jabbed him in the toe. The hook he had tied had speared him in the toe! The right big one and because his arm had become entangled in the line when he reached up he forced the hook in quite deep. Luckily it was only a small hook like the one in his bottom. He remembered the larger hooks he had brought as well. Dam turned around on the ladder and pulled his leg up and whimpered a little from the pain. A drop of blood fell on the platform as he pulled the hook this way and that. It too was firmly embedded.

Undaunted he stood up with his toe hanging over the side. He rummaged in the wet basket and found his lunch which was only wet on one corner, though the lettuce was wet. He found another hook and another mullie worm. He felt for the mullie he'd put in his mouth and he couldn't find it.

Dam sniffed and swallowed, maybe he'd eaten it? He sniffed again and popped the other mullie under his lip. With his mullie tucked away he began to feel like a fisherman again.

It was very awkward balancing on the sloping platform so he tried kneeling, on one leg to give his left leg some relief. He baited his small line and lowered it in the water. No bites. He watched as the small fish swam about the bait.

They simply weren't interested. Dam pulled the line up and took the mullie from his mouth. It moved slightly. He put it on the hook and it wriggled considerably. He dropt it down in front of the fish and, bang! He caught a fish!

With a big smile and a cry of joy he raised it up to the platform and put it in the basket where it flapped about. Dam hastily got all the other mullies out of the bag and stuffed them in his mouth to try to revive them. This became uncomfortable as he began to salivate. After a while he simply couldn't stand it so he spat half of them out and stuffed them up his nose!

"That's better" he said. Almost immediately he could feel them regaining their vitality. Dam quickly rummaged about in his fishing basket for his big line. The tide was high enough now for the big fish to be on the prowl so he wanted to be quick. He found his large line and a great big sinker for he wanted to cast out a long way. He found a large hook and put the little fish on to it.

"Oh if I could only sit down!" he said. Taking the large spool of the hand line in his left hand he began to twirl the bait fish round and round his head.

The more speed the further it would go. Faster and faster it spun, the giant sinker picking up speed like a veritable meteor going about the sun. The line reached a high pitched whistle, then he let go.

All Dam remembered seeing was the fish break free of the hook and land in the water a great distance away then his left arm was pulled violently forward, then "zit!" and a sharp pain in his right ear! Then the image of the sinker flying out in front of him and slowing then rushing back with increasing speed to hit him fair in the chest with a heavy thud - nearly knocking him over!

It then bounced on the platform, bounced once or twice above the water. With each bounce Dam's head responded as did the pain in his ear.

Some moments later he realised the hook had pierced his ear lobe and the weight of the sinker was making his ear lobe longer! He grabbed the line and his head bounced upright! He fumbled for the knife and cut the line and the sinker plopped in the water. With great difficulty Dam tried to pull the giant hook out of his ear lobe. But like the other two, it didn't want to come out!

Dam crouched down on his knees. The tide was coming in and the waves were not far below him. He could still see the little fish below so he found another small hook and put that on the small line again and felt in his mouth for a mullie. They'd all gone! Maybe he'd spat them all out when he was hit in the chest by the sinker? He couldn't remember swallowing them, but he didn't feel hungry.

Dam sniffed automatically and a few mullies slid into the back of his throat from his nose.

"Arh!" he said for he'd forgotten he'd put some there. It turned out to be a very convenient mullie dispenser. All he had to do was sniff and cough and a little mullie would come out of his mouth.

He baited the line and pretty soon had another little fish flapping about in his basket. Eventually Dam caught three, some got away and he'd lost some bait. He snorted and sniffed but no more mullies came out.

The tide was nearing high or so he hoped, for the waves were occasionally splashing his feet. He decided then to eat this lunch because if the tide came up any higher his lunch would become well and truly wet. He sat down with the hook in his bottom sticking well over the edge. He opened his lunch and began eating. The salt water had permeated through all the sandwiches. He ate them all anyway, he hated to see good food wasted. The lettuce tasted quite nice he thought.

As he was eating he noticed some fins come quite close to the pod.

There were big fish quite close! Hurriedly he prepared the fly rod and taking a bright feathered lure from his hat he tied it onto the line. He stood up and slipped. His left leg had become numb from kneeling. He rubbed it as pins and needles shot down to his knee.

With great difficulty he managed to stand on one leg and cast the line.

But just then the handle of the real fell in the water! He watched it tap the bottom rung of the ladder on its way to the bottom. Dam said damn as he placed the rod in its support and got down to his knees. Using the landing net he tried to reach the handle which he could just see glinting on the bottom.

However it was way too short. Talking his shirt off he stepped awkwardly down the ladder into the water. He pulled himself down using the metal frame.

The current and the small waves made him aware of each fish hook which was sticking in him for it wiggled them as he moved. He opened his eyes under water and grasped the handle off the bottom and began to pull himself back up the metal frame.

Back on board he screwed the handle tightly onto the reel so this time it would not come loose. Carefully he stood up as the movement of the waves around him made everything a little unsteady.

Backwards and forwards he flicked his line. It took him a little while to remember how to cast the fly but he was well trained. Then all of a sudden his hat flew out in front of him and landed in the water. Dam flicked at it furiously with the fly-line but it slowly sank beneath the waves.

"My fishing hat!" he cried.

Dam kept standing on one leg, he had to - the waves were lapping his toes.

He closed the fishing basket lid and made sure it couldn't be washed off.

As time went by he stood on the sloping platform occasionally on one leg and then painfully on the other, to let the waves roll up to his knee. Time and time again he flayed the water with the fly. He caught nothing. He stopped for a while and just stood there. Fish came all about him. He couldn't get to his lines they were all under water and he'd run out of mullies.

Suddenly something dark caught his eye and he looked down. To his horror there was a huge shark right under the pod. Dam's heart began to pound.

He watched it and knew it was watching him. Then it bumped the pod and Dam could feel the vibration. Quickly he tried to untie the landing net to use as a weapon. But the knot was one of Dam's specials and was too tight. So he plunged his arms beneath the water and opened his basket to look for his knife. As he was doing so the bottle of strawberry jam began to sway to and fro.

He rescued it and put it in his pocket. He'd lost eye contact with the shark and at any moment expected it to lunge at him.

He found something sharp in the basket or at least his fingers did. He pulled his hand up and saw another fish hook had skewered him in the finger.

Dam didn't worry, he felt for the knife. When he finally found it and had cut the landing net free he stood on one leg with the rod under one arm and the landing net under the other. Up there above the waves he was ready to challenge the monsters of the deep.

The shark had disappeared and Dam found he had cut his middle finger, the same finger with the hook in it.

Dam stood on top of his lopsided pod on one leg. With his knife and rod in the hand with the fish hook in it and with his landing net in the other. With a big hook through his earlobe, a hook in his bottom and one in his big toe and the blood from his finger dripped in the water.

He stood that way for a long time sniffing and breathing, sniffing and breathing.

Finally the tide receded sufficiently for him to be able to sit down, first on his legs with his bottom over the side and then on his knees. He was wet through. Gradually his basket emerged from the sea and he hung the landing net off the side of the pod. Then he cut a strip of cloth from his shirt and bandaged his cut finger.

He felt a little queasy, either sea-sick or hungry he couldn't tell which, so he reached for the strawberry jam. He used his right hand to pull it from his pocket and his right hand again to ladle it into his mouth. He loved strawberry jam.

The tide was half way down the pod when he'd finished and then without warning he was violently sick in the water. Strawberry jam, lettuce, fruit cake, bacon and egg and banana sandwiches and a whole lot of half-digested mullies covered the water. In no time at all the water was alive with fish first little ones and then big ones, all came in and had a feast!

Dam was never one to give up so he began flicking the water with his fly- line. He felt sure he'd catch something and sure enough he had a massive strike! His rod suddenly bent double and began to fly upwards! He'd caught a sea eagle!

Seagulls had come about and were diving in the water to catch the fish.

The sea eagle had swooped and accidentally been hooked by Dam's line.

Up and up it flew. Dam did not know what to do. He decided to bring it down to earth and see if he could get the hook out. After much effort the eagle sat on the water and Dam was able to talk to it and calm it down. The bird seemed to understand what Dam wanted and quietly let Dam take the hook out of its beak. Dam looked in its wild eye and found a friend. But then Dam sniffed and frightened it. The eagle spread its wings and let out a small cry. Much to Dam's relief the great bird took to the air unharmed.

Dam looked below. The fish had disappeared. The tide had gone down sufficiently for Dam to step off his pod and touch the sand. He wasn't scared about sharks anymore; he just wanted to get home. The sun had nearly set.

He carried his rod, net and basket along with a one legged hobble up onto the sand then went back for the pod. With a great effort he pulled it out of the sand and put it over his shoulder. When he was half way to his basket something massive clobbered him on the head! He was knocked clean out and the pod came down on top of him.

He regained consciousness a short while later back up next to the bait shop. He'd been rescued by another fisherman. He was surprised and asked,

"What happened?" as he saw a huge fish lying beside him.

"The sea eagle must have liked you!" said the bait man. "It gave you a present!"

Dam looked at the fish he didn't believe the man. The fish seemed too large for a bird to lift! But then Dam felt the back of his head and there were scales all over his neck and shoulders.

"You're in a mess!" said the bait man looking at all Dam's fish hooks and he kindly offered to clean the fish for him. As he was cleaning it he called out,

"Hey, look at this!" He had found Dam's hat inside the fish's belly!

Dam had a smile as broad as his hat or from his good ear to his bad ear!

He drove himself to horse-piddle to have all the fish hooks removed. When he reached home it was dark.

Covered in bandages and sniffing, Dam sat down to enjoy his fresh fish meal. The sea had given him a fish after all, even though he had really caught himself!

12

Dam Visits the Tip

One morning Dame rose early and since the smell of the air was so fresh and the sun so cheery he decided that day to visit the tip to drop off some rubbish and find some surprises for his "structural adventures" as he liked to call them.

The tip was a long way away on the other side of town. It opened early so the earliest people could find the best surprises.

He quickly ran around the house collecting junk and throwing it into the back of his car. He found a burnt out lawn mower without a petrol tank. Next he found an old washing machine some silly person (Dam) had tried to make into a steam engine. Along the way he filled three large bags of plastic rubbish - old lids and old buckets. He didn't throw much out.... much. Sooner or later, if it was structural, Dam would find a use for it or rather it would find a use for Dam.

It was much more fun to collect things, junk especially thought Dam. Often a trip to the tip usually ended with more coming home than he threw out!

Dam didn't like to think that he may have been addicted to junk, even though it was hard to get rid of sometimes!

The car was full and he was off. The first thing to happen was a puppy dog decided to waltz across the road in front of his car. Dam swerved somewhat and a number of bits of junk moved to one side of the car.

Then the first traffic light Dam came to was red….then the next one and the next. Dam kept checking his mental pocket-watch. And would you believe the next light was red too! When he finally arrived at the tip after the twenty third red traffic light, he was feeling as though he should have stayed in bed!

The air stank! But when he read the sign on the gate that the tip was closed on that particular Sunday, he was not pleased at all! He went up to the tall wire enclosure, grasped the fence and peered across at the luscious pile of waste.

The next time he went he had his dates correct and this time there were only twenty two traffic lights which were red! And this time Dam was one of the first in the queue. He approached the care-taker who looked like a seagull,

"Don't tip anything over there," and "stay outa there!" he yelled, pointing to a great pile of junk. Then pointing in a different direction again he said,

"Go over there!"

Dam went "over there" to a spot where there was not much junk at all!

He peered across to the large pile and immediately with his binocular vision, saw wheels and pulleys, bits of iron, old sewing machines and bicycles.

Just what he needed and before he knew what was happening his car had driven him over to the treasures!

Dam stood before a massive tower of garbage. His mind began to rattle over like a train out of control. He could see old chairs, mattresses, baseball bats and stuffed dolls, cars and old roofing iron - a mountain of delight!

Dam looked down at his feet and saw he was standing in a pool of nuts and bolts. He quickly filled his pockets up until they were bulging, he could hardly walk! He waddled back to his car and realised he had parked in a pile of rusty iron. Fearing a flat tyre he moved the car further around the heap.

As Dam pulled up he saw at the bottom of the pile a pair of lawn mower wheels just like the ones he was looking for! He leapt out of the car and forgetting his pockets were full did a fast waddle-walk over to the wheels.

They were solid and did not want to move being joined to something further in the pile.

Dam pulled and pulled and they moved a little but not enough. He was wondering what to do next when he spied a whole lot of washers and more nuts on the ground. He quickly bent down and picked up as many as he could jamming some into his back pockets.

Dam went to his car and offloaded his junk. He remembered his rope in the boot so he set about attaching it to the wheels and then to the front of his car. Dam was going to get those wheels no matter what!

He began backing the car and the wheels moved. He revved his engine and accelerated. For a moment he thought he was in the wrong gear for all the junk suddenly hurtled towards him and crashed and banged about his car! He then realised he had actually caused a junk-a-lanche, like an avalanche.

Everything went black. The crashing ceased. Dam looked out the windscreen, he couldn't see his wheels anywhere. He tried to open the door but it was jammed. After a little time he said,

"Somebody will find me. Somebody would have noticed!"

He called out a few times for help. Then he thought there may not be enough air in the car for him to breathe so he pondered what to do.

"Nobody knows I'm in here" he said to himself. "But they must be going to level this mound of junk sometime" he thought.

After a length of time he decided to play the radio and turn it up really loud in the hope that it would attract attention. He found a large piece of metal out the window and began to bang in time to the music. Dam made such a noise he had to jam some rags in his ears!

After what seemed like a great length of time he grew impatient and decided to settle for silence. There he sat buried alive and he mused that in years to come perhaps they would find him curled up in his car surrounded by junk!

Dam could hear a noise and sat up to listen more intently. It sounded like someone tapping - no scratching. They sounded a long way away but no they were right there outside Dam's window! He banged the side of the car and the rat moved off through the dense black interior.

Well thought Dam if a rat can crawl through that so can I. He noticed he still had air to breathe so he reckoned the clear day was not so far away. He wound down the window and began pulling bits and pieces into his car until it was pretty full and he had a small space to crawl out into.

Dam turned his radio on, emptied all his pockets of nuts and bolts and head first pushed out into the black space and began to merge with the rubbish.

He found that some of it moved and some didn't. He pushed out and up into the heart of the garbage. Dam was a trained speleologist and was not afraid of the dark smelly spaces of a garbage tip, so he felt somewhat in his element. As he clawed and squeezed his way in the dark he could hear his car radio some meters below him playing green-sleeves.

He pondered the strange reality he now found himself in. The garbage was warm, the great pile was digesting itself. Dam hoped it would not digest him!

Some distance further he became stuck, something had hold of him and was tearing off his pants! Dam reluctantly had to tear his pockets off and in other places his clothes were torn. Further on Dam found the going a little tough.

First he lost his shirt, then half his hair was torn out and something jabbed him in the eye! He had lost the car noise and began to wonder which way was up and which way was down! There were some obstacles which had to be negotiated around some requiring a change of direction to do so.

Dam had been climbing a considerable length of time. He didn't quite know how long. He had been hungry a few times but struggled on. Now it seemed he was truly stuck. One leg was out straight and the other bent backwards, doing the splits in the middle of the garbage pile. The rest of him was quite comfortable except for his arm which became stuck in an upright position.

Dam rested in this position. And in a moment fell asleep.

Dam dreamed he was at sea in a storm the wind was beating hard and the rain was driving in sideways. Dam was not in a ship however he was in a London bus. The bus was swerving to miss dogs and people and kept driving through red lights. The windshield wipers kept sweeping down. Dam's arm kept fidgeting off to the right and suddenly he realised he was the driver of the bus with all those lives on board which he was responsible for. Dam stared out in front trying to find the safest path through the melee. It was no use he had never driven a double-decker bus before - it was Dams trip into hell!

The bus was out of control and approaching a steep descent. The engine began to roar with speed, then suddenly a blinding light and voices. Dam was sure he had heard someone say,

"What the damn hell have we got here?"

Dam woke up he did not know whether he was right side up or down!

There were two people talking somewhere. His leg was stuck up in the air!

"Help," he whispered as he could hardly speak!

"That shoe fooled me!" said one of the men, they hadn't heard Dam. Dam yelled as loud as he could for he still could not move.

"I thought I was seeing things when this leg sticks up out of the bucket, another dead body said I. But then I saw it had a shoe and it looked kinda fresh!"

"Help!" yelled Dam.

"Cripes, it's alive!" came the reply. "Lower the bucket!" Dam was lowered to the ground. The men peered over the edge of the bucket at Dam's leg which didn't move. Quickly they uncovered Dam saying things like,

"It's attached!" and "the original man!" Poor Dam had to be helped from the front end loader onto the ground. One leg was a little bent but the other stuck straight out in front. His arm seemed dislocated.

"What a useless thing!" thought Dam as he tried to move it.

The men helped him over to a seat in the shade. He found he had to keep moving his arm or it would fall asleep. Dam felt quite alright, though a little dirty. He worked out from what they said that he had been crawling around in the rubbish heap for a day and a night.

"You're lucky we got you out in one scoop" they laughed. Dam laughed too. His leg was resting on a tin. He laughed at that also.

"If you find my car," he said "I'd like it back!"

Fortunately for Dam the caretaker gave him enough money to catch a bus home. And even drove him down to the bus stop. In the car Dam had to sit in the back seat and rest his leg on the back of the front seat.

He had a lot of difficulty getting on the bus and when finally his leg was pointing the way home everybody on the bus huddled together as Dam stunk so much. He had borrowed an oversize shirt off a worker and his pants were shredded and filthy and he seemed to have an uncontrollable right arm!

Several days later they uncovered Dam's car and since his uncontrollable leg and arm had ceased their "structural adventures" he caught the bus through twenty three green lights to the tip! His little blue car was not damaged and much to Dam's delight in the back of it was a pile of junk, a coil of rope and a couple of lawn mower wheels. And underneath all that were lots of nuts, bolts and washers!

Dam was very pleased. However he was more careful in the future about what he found and brought home. His passion for the tip had diminished slightly.

13

Dam and the Caterpillars

Dam Diligent had a fascination for insects. He used to dress like them with strange bottle tops for eyes and leaves from the garden for ears and feelers made from water reeds. His neighbours were quite used to seeing him dressed as a grass-hopper mowing the lawn. Once upon a time he made an elaborate costume and dressed up as a huge black cock-roach. However on the way to the fancy dress party he had a severe altercation with a pest control expert.

Dam was intrigued by spiders and would often find himself in the garden after rain watching tiny spiders make bridges and nets across pathways. He kept a spider in a box once and made a little dress for it out of rose petals. When a friend came Dam said he had discovered a new species of spider. Once he found a dead lizard and fashioned a pair of wings for it out of some silk cloth, spider's webs and twigs. He called it his dragon and people believed him when he said it drank some cold water and died!

Dam could make noises like crickets and would sit outside in the dark chatting away. He believed he was talking to them and more than once a big frog had come up to him expecting a meal. Dam had a pet preying-mantis and often fed it cucumber as it sat on the pot-plant on his veranda. Dam would approach it slowly with jerking movements and the mantis would swivel its head from side to side. Dam said it was communicating but people said it was really saying, "Oh no, not cucumber again!"

Then one day Dam found it dead under the plant, lying on its back with its legs in the air. He shed a little tear, it was his only friend. He buried it where it lay and made a small cross for it out of twigs and spider's web. And for a while Dam too became a praying mantis and prayed for his mantis.

When Dam found dead insects in his garden he would bring them home and put them in a box after painting varnish on them to preserve them. When he had a reasonable collection he would perform insect-surgery by taking some glue and sticking butterfly's wings on caterpillars or spider's legs on beetles.

He had quite an unusual collection and would often attach one of his new specimens to his clothing when he went shopping. Quite often he would be the first served in a queue especially when he wore his funnel-web with yellow-petal dress.

One of Dam's favourite hats was an old straw one which had many dead caterpillars hanging from it. It was his special hat for barbeques as it kept the 'Orse-trailor' (Australian) flies away as Dam said.

Dam had a passion for lizards in his youth. One old blue-tongue which was quite tame used to live in the top pocket of his coat. He fed it snails and carried it everywhere slung over his shoulder while he hung onto its tail. The snails he'd keep in his pockets. One day Dam was ordered off a bus because his blue- tongue lizard took a distinct dislike for an old lady with blue hair. It was quite too much for the lady seeing the lizard rear up on its front legs, hiss and stick out its huge blue tongue! For a while it was the lizard verses the handbag so Dam being diligent with his lizard, jumped out a window.

Dam developed an intense dislike for people who collected and killed insects. His worst fear was that a butterfly collector would come prancing through his garden one morning. Dam kept a giant net on a stick behind his door just for the occasion and I hate to think what he would have done with the person once he'd caught them if someone had come along!

Dam had a pet blow-fly which he kept on a string in his pocket. The blue-tongue and the fly were not friends. Some days Dam took one or the other out, never together. The fly had learnt to balance on the edge of his pocket. One time in the bank it decided to have some exercise and leapt off his pocket and landed on the teller's nose!

The poor lady received such a shock the alarm went off and the rest of the bank-staff went pale white and stood motionless, as though they'd been fly-blown. Dam left the bank in a kind of hurry pursued by a strange highly excited piece of string which he kept saying "Naughty! Naughty!" to. Later he thought with a bit of practice he may be able to get the fly to hold up the bank as it had such a numbing effect on the people.

Dam occasionally found 'aromatic bugs' as he called stink-bugs. He noticed the peculiar effect these had on people in restaurants. He would always be served a meal well in advance of anybody else and the waiters never came to close.

He remembered one candle-light supper when a lady friend and he were out on the veranda. Some days earlier Dam had found a luminous stink-bug which glowed in the dark and was particularly aromatic. It let off pungent smells when it was squeezed. It would also hiss and squeal depending on how hard one pressed it.

On this enchanted evening Dam kept it hidden in his top pocket and was so enamoured by its scent that he believed his lady friend would find Dam irresistible.

During the meal his friend wanted a drink of water so Dam filled her glass with rain water. In this glass he dropt a mint leaf. As he was bending low over the table to fill her glass he patted his chest gently and little hisses came from his top pocket. Dam took a deep breath he was feeling terribly romantic. But the woman turned away and coughed. While her head was turned the stink-bug, which was tired of being in Dam's top pocket and probably terribly thirsty, took a flying leap and landed in her glass of water where it rolled over and hid beneath the mint leaf. Dam wafted back into his seat. The woman feeling her throat constrict took several large gulps of water. Of course she swallowed the bug which fortunately for it, managed to grip the back of her tongue with all its six legs and hung on hissing, squealing and stinking! On hearing the commotion Dam hurriedly looked in his top pocket then leapt to the woman's aid.

Holding her head back he jammed his fingers down the poor woman's throat where they danced about for quite some time trying to clasp the insect with two fingers. It let out a tremendous squeal and sprayed aroma everywhere and went in further!

Dam withdrew his hand quickly and to both their surprise the lady's false- teeth came out clamped to Dam's hand! Dam had never seen anything like that before and got quite a shock! He automatically flicked his hand and the false-teeth flew off the veranda into the bushes below. The woman gasped for breath and dared not drink another drop of water!

She'd swallowed it! Dam looked at her in stunned silence, it wasn't her lips that he was looking at! He had an alarmed expression on his face while she retained her integrity! Then the lady quite expectantly let out several unpronounceable expletives and raced downstairs with apologetic Dam in hot pursuit.

When outside the night was black and Dam could hear her mumbling about somewhere in the undergrowth. He sniffed the air. All of a sudden there was an ear piercing shriek and Dam scrambled into the blackness in the direction of the noise.

Through the dense night he came upon her, her hands were clasping her movable mouth as she saw on the ground the ethereal light of the luminous stink-bug as it glowed mysteriously from inside the splendour of her false-teeth!

When Dam placed the insect back in his top pocket, she was horrified. In fact she left rather rudely Dam thought.

Over the years Dam found that he could tell what the weather was doing by studying the insects. The ants for instance would become active before rain and a certain species of beetle would come into the light at night. Dam would telephone the local radio station and tell them what the weather was going to do and most often he was right and they were wrong.

One time his pet Benjamin beetle suddenly started doing hand stands across the table and then falling on its back. It did this several times and Dam pondered the meaning of such antics. Suddenly it hit him quite literally for there was an earthquake and several books fell from the shelf and squashed poor Benjamin! As Dam lifted the book, slowly he was surprised to see that it was a book on Yoga!

"Oh Benjamin!" he cried, "You've stretched yourself this time!"

One dry day Dam was in his backyard when he came upon a trail of hairy caterpillars all in a line. It was the first time Dam had ever seen a trail like that before and he sat down and watched them with childlike curiosity. The line stretched some six meters and involved one hundred and fifty three caterpillars!

The caterpillar in the lead looked like all the rest. And with their noses to the tail in front, the line looked like one big long grub. Dam looked very closely at the one in front to see if it wasn't special in some way.

Dam had a plan. He took the leading caterpillar and put it at the end of the line to see what would happen but they all kept in line walking, so he put it back up the front. Then he took the one from the rear and put it up the front and they all kept in line walking as usual. So Dam took two caterpillars from the front and put them at the rear. After some time they found the end of the line and kept walking. So Dam took three caterpillars from the front and put them at the rear and still they kept walking! Next Dam took three caterpillars from the rear and put them up front and still the line of grubs went hobble-de-hobble as caterpillars do!

Dam's plan of course was to find out why they were following each other.

He thought that one of them may be more intelligent and not want to follow the leader.

After several days of caterpillar moving Dam concluded his intense research. He decided that the grubs were highly intelligent and that each of them was capable of being the leader. Dam discovered this many days later as he'd moved each caterpillar over one thousand times!

This was one of the most difficult things Dam had ever done since quite often he'd lost count and because all the caterpillars looked the same he had to start counting all over again!

14

Dam and the Vegetable Garden

Dam watched the white clouds dancing in the blue. It was spring at last and time to plant seeds. He was pretty sure it was spring, the birds knew. He had bought a clock for the first time in his life. Before that he knew the time by the roll of the day and the singing of the birds.

The next day found him digging in his vegetable garden when somebody's arm popped up amongst the beans. Dam looked the other way, he thought he was seeing things. No, it was still there! The hand looked fresh so he bent down to shake it as if to say "How do you do?"

As he took hold of it he noticed it was quite cold. No - somebody wasn't hiding in his bean patch, somebody had been buried there! Dam looked around momentarily forgetting where he was. Yes it was his vegetable patch!

Dam heaved on the arm with all his might and lo a beautiful woman emerged from the earth and lay there before him as fresh as a daisy. Dam was shocked.

"Where have you been all my life?" he said rubbing his eyes and looking around again. He quickly felt for her heart beat but there was none. How could she have crept in and died beneath his beans? Dam was perplexed, he picked a few leaves and tried to cover her nudity. Then he raced inside to ring the police.

Presently the police came and tried to identify the person. They took her photograph with Dam standing beside his bean patch with two huge naked feet in front. Dam was not smiling. They took her away and Dam was almost sorry to see her go.

Several weeks later he was told that the woman had been missing for twenty years! Her name was Lucy and she had died of a mysterious disease twenty years ago. Nobody could identify the disease as her body went missing and they were unable to diagnose the illness.

Dam reckoned somebody was playing a joke on him and had come into his bean patch in the night and dug a hole after getting Lucy out of the fridge!

He was sure she wasn't in there when he planted the beans, or was she?

He tried to remember when he'd planted them. Perhaps they were as old as Lucy?

The next day he read the papers and there on the front page was Dam in his bean patch. You couldn't see Lucy though, she was hidden by her feet.

The caption read, "Bean a long time under."

Dam wasn't smiling. The paper said they were doing tests on her to find out why she died.

Dam went outside to water his beans. These were no ordinary beans.

They were diligent beans planted by Dam Diligent himself. Already they were over a meter high and were growing fifteen centimetres a day!

"Maybe Lucy had eaten some beans?" he thought.

Dam kept his eyes on the newspaper. Then one day a report came through that Lucy was found to have high levels of preservatives in her body. And that she had probably died of hyper-preservititis a disease caused by eating genetically modified beans. This startling evidence seemed to indicate that her body was snatched up by the bean producers and taken to a remote location like Dam's backyard and buried. Dam's mind began to wonder, he looked around to bring himself back to reality.

"Too many preservatives," he said to himself as he watered his two metre high beans.

"I wonder if these beans will have the same effect on me?" he said.

The newspapers soon became filled with complaints from other sources, especially the morgue where dead people went to be analysed. They were finding that many people were being preserved. People who'd been dead ten years were still as fresh as daisies – their bodies weren't rotting. One male soya bean eater like Lucy, had been dead for three years and was still fresh and sweet. Some person had to shave him every day!

A great furore erupted in the medical fraternity and Dam was called to go on television and describe what happened in his bean patch that fateful day when he had found Lucy. Dam wasn't smiling and was difficult to film as his head kept moving left and right as he kept looking around.

The government demanded that food producers advise the public if they put preservatives in their foods. This was essential for the government's Duty of Care towards its citizens. For instance a hamburger store was found to use beans and preservatives all at once! One could not buy the preservatives in shops on their own, only hamburgers with preservatives in them. People were dying of hyper-preservititis and the associated gulpin-urrger virus which was linked to hamburgers.

Dam watered his beans they were growing quite large. The government moved to ban all preservatives in food as electricity consumption was going down as people were being preserved without using fridges.

Dam looked sideways up at his new clock. He had come to realise that it never told a lie and for that reason he grew fond of it.

Medical authorities also found a link between large feet and preservatives. The preservatives preserved people as they grew giant feet and was a contributing factor in producing large tall people who needed large shoes!

Shoe factories were found to be in league with pharmaceutical companies.

As a result of finding Lucy, Dam and many other people went shopping and observed all the huge people and wondered why and if they weren't on the way to being hyper-preservitated and gulpin-bugurred as well!

Dam watered his bean patch but it was no use the beans had not begun to flower and already they were three meters high! Dam was sure they too were suffering from hyper-preservititis or gulping-bugurred-isation as he recalled!

Several scientific studies were published in the newspapers and one drew attention to the fact that preservatives enlarged people's ears as well as their feet. Other external physical characteristics such as hair, hands, ears, skin and feet seemed to be preserved however the internal organs were racked with illness and disease and deteriorated in function more rapidly. For example people with large feet could not run of jump faster or higher and people with big ears could not hear any better once their stomachs rotted away. This alarming news was responsible for a rush on hamburger shops as people wanted to experience the truth and feel for themselves.

Dam looked in the mirror. He pulled his ears out and measured them with a ruler. Next he measured his feet and wrote the date and measurements on paper which he stuck on the wall. He wrote the time down as well. He felt his heart beat and couldn't find it, then remembered it was on the other side. He stuck out his tongue it was green with pink spots, quite normal. He shuffled outside to watch his beans grow.

Looking around in the evening light, he stood beneath their waving stems green and twisting far above. High up on the tallest branch Dam noticed the beginnings of a flower.

"I'm not going to eat these beans anyway," he said to himself as he lay in bed.

"I will have to dig them all out!"

That night Dam had a dream that the bean pods grew as large as cricket bats and he hung many up in his kitchen to dry. Several days later there was a loud explosion and a bean-pod released several seeds on the floor but they weren't seeds they were small people, little babies and they all looked like Lucy, he recognised the feet!

Dam raced outside in the morning and found bean pods the size of cricket bats five meters up in the air! He ran and fetched his axe and cut all the beans down. He had a great armful of pods and struggled with them into his kitchen. He tried to cut one open with a knife but it was so hard he had to use his axe. The beans were as large as half bricks and just about as hard.

He rang the newspaper and asked them if they'd heard about huge beans and they came out again and photographed Dam holding a bean seed and a pod. Dam wasn't smiling.

The next day a truck arrived and ten men leapt out with shovels and guns and dug a great hole in his bean patch and much to Dam's amazement found five more perfectly preserved bodies underneath the soil! They threw them in the back of the truck and took off saying they were scientists. They took all Dam's bean-pods as well!

Poor Dam was left with a five meter by four metre hole where his been patch had bean. He began to feel miserable. He went inside and looked in the mirror, stuck out his tongue and measured his ears. It seemed that his left ear had grown two millimetres. He went to bed he was feeling sick. He turned the radio on but he could not hear it even when he turned the sound way up!

Dam woke up with a start. Some idiot had left the radio on full blast!

He jumped out of bed and ran into the kitchen.

There on the sink was an opened can of beans. Dam read the label, "Genetically modified and preservative added." He gasped and ran outside to look at his bean patch and to his great joy it was still there!

It had all been a dream. The beans were only two meters tall and many of them were ready to pick!

He jumped in amongst them and began to eat beans for breakfast. As he was picking them a hand popped out of the branches! Dam received such a shock a bean went down his throat the wrong way. He coughed and spluttered then went back to look at the hand. It was green and looked awfully like the rubber-glove he'd lost three days before! It was the rubber glove Dam had lost three days before!

He kept eating beans. After sometime he went inside, looked at the clock and turned the radio on. He stood in front of the mirror and wiggled his ears. He had a big smile all over his face.

Just then the news came on the radio and the first item was about food preservatives and genetically modified beans! The news reader said that the preservatives actually preserved bodies and the genetic modifications made people's feet and ears grow large! Also preservatives made people lose their sense of direction and time! Dam looked around and then at the clock.

He read the label on the bean tin again. He looked in the mirror and measured his ears again. He went to bed, he was feeling ill. But he soon got up, again.

He spent the rest of the day getting in and out of bed many times as he had severe stomach pains from eating all the beans.

15

Dam Diligent the Lion Tamer

Dam Diligent had a favourite cow. It had large black eyes and huge eyelashes and was udderly fantastic. Every morning he would wake super early, rain or shine and singing his favourite song would open the gate of her yard and proceed to milk her. Dam's cow was called Daisy and her favourite food was daisies. That's why she was kept in a yard for she was crazy for Dam's daisies which he had growing all around the house.

One cold and bleak winter's morning Dam rose early and went outside with his milking bucket. It was so early the sun was not up yet and all his daisies were still asleep with their petals closed. Dam walked around the gate of Daisy's yard and climbed through the fence for a large puddle had formed just on the other side of the gate. He sang his song and Daisy came over to him to be milked.

As he was milking her it began to rain and Dam pulled his coat up around his neck and shivered a little - then he shivered a lot. Daisy was cold too and then and there Dam decided to build Daisy a roof to keep her warm so he could milk her and not get wet. He took his milk back around the mud puddle which was rather large, slipped through the gate and went into his house.

Dam kept his house spotlessly clean and being diligent had a unique method of making butter which he devised over the years. He would hang the bucket from a rope suspended from the ceiling. This he twisted until the bucket was high up and then he'd let go and the bucket would spin furiously until it stopped after going this way and that way for some time. The butter was delicious.

This day, he decided, was the very day to commence work on Daisy's shed! So Dam being diligent set to work immediately. He went and fetched his old anchor rope, his axe and his tractor. His plan was to go up the back of the house and cut a large tree down and pull it down the slope with his very long anchor rope attached to his tractor.

Dam marched up the hill with his axe and rope over one shoulder. The going was tough though Dam was tougher and unlike the bush he was dry. Finally he reached a tree but that was too small. He climbed higher and reached another tree that was larger but still too small. Then he came upon a huge tree just the right size. It took Dam no time at all to chop the tree down. It fell awfully slowly and landed up hill. Fortunately that was just where Dam wanted it to fall and after clearing some branches off the side of it he was ready to tie it up and pull it down the slope.

Now strange as Dam's luck was, the tree was directly behind his house and the only direction it could be pulled was straight through his living room!

Dam started his tractor with a pull-rope and the engine roared like a lion into action. He drove the tractor to the front steps near his daisies and hitched the rope to it. The rope went in the front hallway, past the television set and his favourite chair, past the kitchen and then past the bucket of butter then out onto the back veranda and on up the slope.

Dam climbed aboard the tractor and began to pull the tree down the slope. Everything went well and the tree seemed easy to move. The tractor reached Daisy's gate and stopped in the mud puddle. Dam put it in reverse and after churning up a little mud managed to back it up to the front steps again. He took up the slack in the rope, tied it to the tractor and was off once more pulling the huge tree. The rope strained and finally Dam's tractor made another journey to the mud puddle. When he reached the gate he stopped and began to reverse. Daisy came over to have a look and stood on the other side of the mud puddle.

Dam began to sing. He reversed up to the stairs again tied the rope to the tractor and was off once more. The rope strained and moved a little it strained a lot so Dam revved the engine hard.

Just then there was a tremendous snap and all Dam saw was his beautiful nylon anchor rope whip past his left ear like the tongue of a great snake.

It flew in front of him and collided with poor Daisy. Dam and Daisy received such a shock they both let out a loud shout! Daisy was udderly shattered and took off like a bull. Dam didn't know she could move so quickly! She raced round and round the field moaning in pain and shock. But that was not all, suddenly there was a great crash from behind and Dam turned around just in time to see his favourite chair and his bucket of butter come hurtling through the air with the tree behind. It flew past Dam's right ear with a roar after passing straight through his house and speared straight into the mud puddle! There was a large splash and Daisy stopped running and stood along way off panting.

Dam turned the engine off and walked over to the puddle. His chair was broken and the tree was imbedded in the mud.

The problem was that half the tree was still inside the house because it was so long. So Dam walked up the hill to get his axe and then cut the tree in half.

In no time at all he managed to haul the bit that was inside the house down the front steps. He laid it next to the fence. He tied his broken rope to the piece which had stuck in the puddle and tried to pull it out but it was stuck. He revved up the tractor engine but the tree had speared deep into the ground as though it had replanted itself. He had to chop it down again, it was in the ground so far.

Daisy came closer to watch though not too close. In no time at all the tree was cut down again and Dam dragged it over to the fence with the tractor.

His plan was to split the pieces for Daisy's shed but first he had to dig his chair out of the mud puddle. Poor Dam spent all the rest of that day digging in the mud for he didn't like to muck around being Dam! When he had dug a huge hole he tied the rope around the piece of tree remaining in the hole and pulled it out with his tractor. Out it popped like a splinter being well oiled by the bucket of butter and Dam's chair.

The bucket was flattened and Dam's chair was unrecognisable. He threw both in the hole and watched them sink. Daisy looked on.

Next day Dam was up early and was soon milking Daisy and singing to her.

She closed her eyes but all she could see was a piece of rope flying through the air. Dam used a bit of his anchor rope to spin his bucket of milk to make butter. Then he went outside with his axe and began splitting the logs. In no time at all he had enough planks to build Daisy's shed.

All that week Dam worked and soon the time came to put the roof on.

Dam had no roofing iron so he had to drive into town to buy some. On his way home all the iron blew off the roof of his car as he'd forgotten to tie it on! Fortunately it landed in a park where there were a whole lot of tents.

One of the pieces of iron came to rest next to a small orange tent and Dam crept up and was about to pick up the iron when a great roar came from inside the tent. Dam leapt two meters in the air. A man came around the corner he looked angry like he'd been at the barbers for he had soap on one side of his face

"What are you doing!?" he yelled.

"J…just blew off the roof," said Dam.

"You watch out," said the man.

"I'm the Lion Tamer and there's lions in here!"

"Oh sorry," said Dam and picked up his sheet of iron.

"Are you coming to the circus?" asked the lion tamer.

"Yes please!" said Dam who used to be a trapeze artist in his youth.

"It's on tonight" the man said, and went back to his shaving. He was so hairy Dam thought he had a mane like a lion around his neck. Dam chuckled to himself on the way home and thought the lion tamer would be better off with a lawn mower rather than a razor.

That afternoon Dam put the roof on Daisy's shed and was soon standing inside it with her, patting her on the head and saying,

"Now we won't be cold in the mornings." Dam ate an early dinner and was soon on his way to the circus.

He watched the trapeze act and that was wonderful. He watched the horses and that was even better. He watched the elephants and the clowns and they were better still. Dam laughed out loud when the clowns came out in fact he laughed so loudly everybody turned around and looked at him. But the best act of all was the lion tamer. Dam sat on the edge of his seat and bit his bottom lip he was so scared.

Dam felt sorry for the lion as the angry lion tamer was cracking his whip and roaring like a lion. The lion was angry too and just as the lion tamer was about to put his hairy head in the lions mouth the lion jumped off the chair and bounded for the door of the cage. The lion was intelligent and must have known somebody had left the door unlocked! The lion opened the large door and escaped!

Dam was suddenly surrounded by screaming people. Several young girls and many other people in front of him sprang over the back of their seats and trampled him. He was bruised and scared. When he looked up all he could see was the lion's legs above him and he let out a little whimper. The lion walked straight over the top of Dam whose own legs felt like butter!

After sometime he stood up. People were still running this way and that.

The lion tamer tried to call out but all that came out of him was a loud roaring noise which seemed to make people run faster!

Dam left and crept outside peeping around every corner. The place was deserted. He tip-toed out to his car and took off for home. Already people were calling out 'lions escaped' as he drove down the streets. He cleaned the windscreen and kept an eye out for the lion. That night as he lay awake in bed all he could see was the underbelly of the lion. Dam slept like a log.

Next morning he woke early as usual and having forgotten about the lion fetched his bucket and went out to milk Daisy.

He was still weary as he opened the door of Daisy's new shed and there lying on the floor looking up at him was the lion! Dam jumped like a spark, waking up with a terrible fright.

"Daisy!" cried Dam and the lion looked up, its big soft eyes blinking. "He's eaten Daisy!" he thought and slammed the door and flew back to the house but he fell in the mud puddle which he'd dug out! The mud was soft it had filled up with water and it was quite deep. He found his chair again, dilapidated and mangled, he just managed to stand on its two legs! In the half-light Dam could see Daisy over in the corner of the paddock.

"Help!" cried Dam as though she was human and would understand.

Dam's heart sent ripples through the mud. He was stranded and the mud was cold.

After a desperate effort he jumped off and beating the mud like a butter churn finally reached the shore. He dragged himself out and ran up the front steps of his house into the hallway splattering mud everywhere and picked up the phone. But he put the wrong end of it in his ear. He banged it on the table to get rid of all the mud. The voice at the other end of the phone said,

"Gun shots!" and Dam yelled,

'It's here, the lion is in Daisy's shed!"

The policeman said he'd be right up as soon as possible. Dam had a shower his face was covered in mud. The plug hole spluttered and gurgled as it was clogged and didn't drain too well. Soon a car arrived and six policemen leapt out with guns bristling and helmets on. Then the hairy lion tamer popped out like a cork with a lead and asked Dam where the shed was.

Dam pointed to it and said,

"Mind the mud puddle." The policemen ran up to the house, shut the door and pointed their guns out the windows.

"It's alright" said the lion tamer and asked Dam if he had any butter.

"Butter!" cried Dam and he raced into the kitchen and grabbed the extra bucket from the old anchor rope. "Here" he said.

Dam went up into his house. The lion tamer went across to the shed and tip-toed around the mud puddle. He began to talk to the lion in a low voice as he opened the door. There the lion sat under Daisy's roof. It came forward and began to lick the butter. The lion tamer put the leash around the lion's neck and began to walk back towards the house. But it was too late the lion tamer fell head first in the puddle. Now it was a funny sight and all the policemen began to laugh but soon stopped laughing as they saw that the man could not swim! The lion didn't seem at all interested and sat down to lick the butter.

One policeman quickly jumped out the window and ran around and around in circles yelling,

"Where's a rope?" Dam ran and untied the butter rope from the kitchen and threw it out the window. The policeman raced down and threw it to the lion tamer who promptly pulled him in the mud puddle as well! Another policeman jumped out the window and ran and grabbed the rope but with the two men in the puddle he was pulled in also! Another policeman jumped out the window but he fell off the veranda and limped over to the gate.

"One at a time!" he yelled but slipped and was pulled in too! Then the forth policeman jumped out the window, ran around and around on one side of the puddle waving wildly until he banged into the fence and fell in the puddle as well! The last policeman leapt out of the window. He raced over grabbed the rope. Unfortunately he looked at the lion which looked back at him.

That policeman did a great big belly-flop in the mud puddle amongst them all!

Dam looked out the window. The mud puddle was alive with policemen and helmets and one lion tamer who kept coming up and going down much like the lion's head in the bucket of butter!

Dam opened the front door and bounced upon his tractor like a trusty horse. He reached for the pull-cord and started the engine which roared like a lion.

He backed it up to the mud puddle and tied the rope to the back of it. All at once six muddy policemen popped up out of the hole.

Their pockets were full of mud and they were puffing and spluttering.

When they were out they raced up to the house and shut the door. Their muddy faces looked out the windows. The lion tamer was still coming up and going down in the water. When he came up the lion looked up and when he went down the lion kept licking the butter.

Dam dived into the mud puddle and using all his strength grabbed the lion tamer by the scruff of the neck and hurled him from the puddle with such force that he landed on his feet on the grass! He stood there for a while gasping for breath.

Dam pulled himself out of the mud puddle and began to sing. Daisy came over and looked at the lion with her great big eyes. The lion was looking at Daisy now. Dam still singing squelched over to the lion, picked up its lead and walked carefully around the puddle and took it to the lion tamer. The lion tamer wiped his eyes, blinked and said thank you in a little squeaky voice.

The policemen seeing that the lion was not dangerous put down their weapons and came out onto the veranda.

It was now early morning and the sun was shining brightly and by the time all had shaken Dam's muddy hand the lion truck had arrived and the lion was safely put inside. All the men looked at each other and began to laugh as they were all covered in mud.

Dam said farewell and went inside to have another shower. As he was showering he heard a tap on the bathroom door.

"Now who could that be?" he thought. When he opened the door Daisy was there! She had somehow walked around the mud puddle and up the front steps and into the house. There she stood looking at her friend Dam Diligent the lion tamer. She was chewing a large mouthful of daisies and the hallway was covered in petals and mud.

16

Dam's Damn Dam

Dam had a dam, it was a damn dam and Dam was damned if he was going to let his dam die! For it was clogged with two types of green weed. One was growing on its surface and the other had dug its roots into the muddy bottom; both were very difficult to remove. The green surface weed appeared a few weeks before and Dam eyed it and said not to worry, he'd see to it soon and there was no way Dam was going to let a weed outsmart the old Dam Diligent!

Then it grew and it grew. It grew until the whole surface was seething in weed. It was a horrid green colour and blocked out the blue sky and the slender white reflections of the surrounding tree trunks.

There were fish in Dam's dam. He'd placed them in there as tiny babies and now they were monsters which thrashed the water with their magnificent broad tails. They were so big they ate any duck which settled on the dam and baby ducks were gobbled up hole! Dam didn't mind that as the ducks had brought the weed in on their feathers. Though he did feel sorry for the mother ducks who were only teaching their ducklings to swim.

As he walked around the dam's edge he saw many small creatures such as frogs and dragon flies. He knew the weed would suffocate the fish by taking all the oxygen out of the water so he set about devising methods of extracting the weed from the surface. He couldn't poison the weed that would poison the fish. He couldn't drain the dam that would leave the fish dry. Dam thought it was a pity the fish didn't eat the weed then he wouldn't have to go to so much trouble removing it….somehow!

He launched his boat and paddled out. The weed was so thick his boat hardly moved. He scooped some up and put it in a bucket; he scooped a lot up and put it in his boat. But the weed grew back and filled the space in no time at all.

For the first time in Dam's life he was in a dilemma.

"If I see another duck, I will shoot it!" is what he said!

Sure enough the next day when he was in his boat a duck flew overhead.

Dam clapped his hands and stood up, grabbed a handful of weed and threw it up at the duck. It hit the duck fair in the face so the duck could not see. Dam was such a good shot!

The duck swerved and flew off and Dam fell overboard! He swam to shore and came out with a slimy green hat on. Dam felt green for the rest of that day.

He looked out his kitchen window and believed he could hear his fish gasping for air.

That night he dreamed he was a duck flying over a green forest. Suddenly a great lump of green weed came flying up from the ground and covered his face! He crashed into a tree!

Next day Dam rose early and went straight to work. He twisted a whole lot of metal and wire into an anchor shape and began to throw it out in the water.

As he pulled it in a small amount of weed came with it. It was a slow process and by the afternoon he had dredged only a small amount of the weed onto the bank. But the weed grew back overnight and covered the dam once again. He looked out the window of his kitchen.

"Damn the dam!" said Dam.

Deep in the night he had a dream. He dreamt he was a duck flying over a green forest. Somewhere below him were ducks hunters with green-weed sling shots and green weed was flying through the air all around him. He ducked for cover!

The next day he woke early and made a type of sling shot which consisted of a along piece of rope which had springs at either end, tied between two trees across the dam. Then another rope off from the middle of it which Dam used to draw the spring-rope back with. As he let go the long rope would flick the weed out of the dam. The rope struck the dam like the string of a bow and lots of weed went flying through the air onto the bank.

At the end of the day Dam was so tired he rested on the trigger rope and accidentally pulled the release lever. He forgot to let go of the large rope and in an instant he was violently flung across the water where he engorged several mouthfuls of weed before coming to rest head first in the mud on the opposite bank. Dam went to his kitchen his eyes were full of mud. He stuck his head in the sink.

That night he again dreamed he was a duck flying over a green forest.

The forest was full of vines and each vine looked like the green weed. He felt sick.

Next morning he woke early and went down to the dam to get some weed.

He bought it back to his house and cooked it for breakfast. This made him feel even sicker!

Then he had a plan. He thought it might make a good medicine so he fetched some more, dried it and chopped it up and put it in a bottle.

"If I tell people it will make them feel well, they'll buy it." He dried a whole lot out and said it was a magic medicine. Quite a few people bought it but said it made them sick and they called Dam a 'Quack!'

"You've got to feel sick before you can feel well!" he told them ducking for cover. So they bought some more! Then people began to complain that it was growing in their gardens.

"Nonsense!" said Dam. "It won't grow out of water." Dam went into his kitchen and filled the sink to wash up and something green popped out of the tap! It was the weed!

Dam had had enough. He rang the ambulance (angry-lance) his tap was sick, he rang the police, the weed had stolen his time! He rang the army, the weed was invading people's backyards!

"Help!" he flapped. "This weed is growing out of control!"

The ambulance came, the police came and the army came. They all looked at Dam and agreed he was a little green.

"This should be easy to control!" they said. They looked at Dam and he laughed.

Next day several men arrived in a truck. They began to net the dam with a fine mesh. By the end of the day all the weed was gone. Dam gave them the money he had made from selling the weed as a medicine. He thanked them and they wished Dam well.

That night Dam dreamed he was a duck flying over a dam full of weed. As he looked down he saw someone in a boat throwing weed up at him. He laughed and flew off quacking.

Next day Dam looked out the window of his kitchen and there on the surface of the dam swimming around was a duck and swimming around the duck was a great mass of green weed. It had grown back overnight! Dam raced into town and bought a great big net. He covered the whole dam two meters above the surface with the net. Next he bought a great roll of black plastic and a small pump. The plastic he placed all over the weed and the pump he placed on the bank so it pumped air under the plastic.

For three days the pump ran hot and the water bubbled under the plastic.

At the end of the three days Dam went down to the plastic and peeped underneath. The weed had gone. It had all died from lack of light.

Dam delightedly removed the plastic. It had worked. Now the ducks could not bring any weed in and he had eradicated all traces of it. Dam went up to his kitchen and ran the tap. Green weed poured out of it into the sink. Dam looked on in astonishment.

Just then there was a knock on the front door. When Dam opened it he found there was a small person standing there. He was dressed like a duck with long pointed shoes and a very round hat which stuck out a long way in the front.

The man had a little bottle of green weed in his hand and said in a little voice,

"This is green medicine, it will cure any illness you have!" The man was desperate to sell Dam the bottle. Dam smiled and said,

"Quack! Quack!" and closed the door.

17

Dam Finds God

Once Dam made a rocking chair out of sticks and before he'd finished making it he tried it out and fell off the veranda backwards and nearly broke his neck! He still sits in it, however he is afraid to lean too far back and he doesn't let it rock anymore, now that he's given it an extra leg.

He sits in it sometimes and watches the day pass by. He often thinks he should be doing something more useful so he spends a lot of time sitting there wondering just what he could or should be doing.

One day as he was staring at his toe nails watching them grow and thinking about himself thinking, he heard a voice in the street below. It was the soft voice of a woman singing and Dam's ears pricked up into special hearing mode. Through the trees he caught the sight of a lone figure walking along who seemed to be talking to herself for there was nobody else around. Dam watched with binocular vision and to his intrigue saw that the woman was followed by a large pack of dogs.

Dam had heard about this 'Lady with the Dogs,' so he jumped up and walked down to the bottom of his driveway to get a closer view. As she drew near he could see she was carrying a small puppy and singing. She was wearing a white dress with pale blue flowers all over it and looked extremely beautiful.

Dam was quite transfixed and stood staring, his mouth open. The lady saw him and kept walking. The dogs saw Dam too and came bounding up to him and with little warning began growling and attacking him. One of them lunged at his legs and another bit him on the arm. Dam received quite a shock and shot up the nearest tree.

The lady with the dogs stopped singing and came to call off the dogs.

She was most apologetic and begged Dam's forgiveness. He sat up in the tree and looked down at her. Her hazel eyes and soft voice were talking but Dam seemed to be in another world. Slowly he climbed down.

"They weren't attacking you, they were playing, they only do that to people they like," is what she said. Dam looked at his arms and legs to see if he wasn't bleeding.

"I am sorry, they get a bit carried away sometimes," she continued. Dam was well and truly carried away.

"I like dogs," he said. And before he knew what was happening the lady had thrust the little puppy she was holding into Dam's arms.

"Here" she said, "is a present." Dam looked down at the little ball of fluff. And two large brown eyes peered back up at him.

"Oh" said Dam, "I .."

"You need a friend" the lady said, "and the little puppy needs a good home and likes you!"

All the other dogs came about, they were wagging their tails. He looked into the ladies smiling face and could not say anything. He looked down at the little puppy and smiled. Dam had found a friend.

"Thank you," he said and asked if she was walking that way tomorrow.

She replied that she would be around sometime.

Dam walked up his driveway with the puppy in his arms and angels in his heart. As he was walking he began to softly sing and to his wonder the little dog sat up and began to howl as well! They both sat down on the veranda in the rocking chair and soon the little puppy fell asleep. It was a little girl dog with long eyelashes, big brown eyes and long soft brown and white fur. She had floppy ears, a short little nose, a small white beard and a fluffy tail which curled up over her back. She was very tiny and fitted neatly in Dam's two hands.

Over the next few weeks Dam fed her and washed her. He played with her by tying his best socks on a string and pulling them along the floor. The little dog always wanted to sleep in Dam's bed with him. She would crawl down to his feet and keep them warm.

Dam didn't need to train her. She knew what was right and what was wrong. The only thing she did which annoyed him, was steal his tools when he was working on the car. She'd take them away secretly and bury things like nuts and bolts which the car needed to go. At first Dam thought he'd misplaced them, then one day he noticed the little dog looking guilty so Dam said,

"Oh, ho, what have you got there?" The little dog stopped and looked up at him then dropt the small screwdriver on the floor.

No matter how hard Dam thought, he simply couldn't come up with a name for his little dog. She seemed like an unusual animal and Dam was quite concerned about a name but in the meantime he simply called her "Little Dog."

Little Dog followed Dam everywhere around the house and around his orchard. Sometimes he'd take her on long afternoon walks up the mountain and back which was a difficult walk for a little dog. Then down to the nearby creek.

She was great company for him and kept him laughing at unexpected moments and she was always interested in what Dam was up to. And for a while Dam's toe nails actually stopped growing!

One day they were in the orchard picking up macadamia nuts. The little dog was fascinated in their round shape and chased them when Dam rolled them.

Later that day he was cracking them open and gave some to his little friend. She wolfed them down hungrily and came back for more.

Later that night the little dog suddenly let out an agonised howl of pain.

Dam was asleep and woke up with a start. He quickly helped her up and asked her what was wrong. Little Dog whimpered and muzzled up to Dam, then unexpectedly began to howl again.

"Oh what is wrong Little Dog?" he said in distress. "Have you got pain in your tummy?" The little dog was in agony and began to howl and cry. It arched its back as though something was stuck in its stomach. Dam began to think that the nuts were poisonous or were stuck in her stomach. He began to think it was his fault she was in such pain. He stroked her tummy and tried to comfort her.

All night the little dog howled and Dam couldn't get any sleep. He tried to give her some water to drink thinking it would help her digest the nuts.

Finally he managed to sleep a little but soon woke and realised the little dog had gone.

He jumped out of bed and looked around the house. Fearing the worst he grabbed a torch and raced outside. The night was crisp and cold and the stars were out. Where had she disappeared to?

He looked under the house and around the yard, she was nowhere. In his mind's eye he could see her lying under a tree dying of agony. Dam began to walk down the driveway and along the road. He searched the creek some distance towards town. Maybe he would find her there as dogs usually go to water to die. He shone the torch up and down the creek banks and into the clear water. There were no tracks in the mud and no other signs. Dam retraced his steps, he looked everywhere they had walked except up the mountain. He began to whistle and call. He flashed the torch up and down the road but there was no sound or sign of his little dog. Dam was very upset and thought she had already died.

With a heavy heart he retraced his steps and began to look more closely around the house. He looked on the veranda and in the rocking chair. He looked under the car and under every tree in the orchard including the macadamia tree. Still no sign. He looked up at the mountain. No, she did not have the strength to climb up there.

Then he heard a screeching noise, it was coming from the house. He raced up the veranda steps and listened again. Maybe she was still in the house!

He began to look under every shelf and in every corner, after all she was still quite small and could hide anywhere.

Dam found her eventually. She was still in the bed!

She had crawled down under the blankets and was asleep in a corner. Dam held her very close and stroked her poor sore tummy. Gradually Dam's little dog fell asleep with Dam's big arm around her. Both of them slept in the next day.

As Dam slept he had a terrible dream. He dreamt he was walking on a beach in a very hot wind. In the sand were many footprints of dogs. The wind was so strong he could barely stay upright. As he watched the waves he noticed a large orange cloud far away above the horizon. Out of the cloud came a long red spiralling flame. It struck the sea and all the waves turned into flames.

Just then Dam heard cries from the sea and looking out saw a lady in distress battling with the waves. Then the wind overcame him and he was hurled along the beach and into the flames. He swam out and as he came nearer to her he realised it was the lady with the dogs. He could see the cloud coming nearer and nearer and all at once Dam and the lady were lifted into the sky at tremendous speed. They went way way up beyond the cloud and entered a vast black space.

Almost at once a strange figure with large brown eyes and a long white beard approached the lady with a glass of water which she half drank. The figure tried to get Dam to drink from the glass too but Dam didn't understand why and didn't feel thirsty. The figure then threw the water over Dam and he realised he was on fire!

Dam woke up. His little dog was licking his face.

"Argh! No!" he cried, pushing his little friend away. "Oh!" he said realising it was a dream.

"You saved my life, and you survived too, I'm going to call you God!" he said, "which after all is Dog spelt backwards!"

With that they both jumped out of bed, God grabbed one of Dam's socks and raced into the kitchen. And the first thing they both did was have a long drink of water.

Dam hardly found time anymore to sit in his rocking chair and study his toe nails. He found God's toe nails grew so quickly he had no time to relax and seemed to be always cutting hers!

18

Dam goes Opal Mining

When Dam lived in the city he used to ride his bicycle to work each day across the Harbour Bridge. These days though the city was a smoggy place and not very clean so he donned a gas-mask which made some people laugh and pedestrians get out of his way. Dam could pedal his bicycle as fast as any car even down stairs for at the end of the bridge there were several flights of stairs he used to go down. Not on the stairs themselves but in the middle right next to the hand railing where there was a flat spot twenty centimetres wide.

One day Dam was half a second late and he did his normal forty kilometres per hour crossing of the bridge and his usual ninety degree turn at the end of it to go down the seventy degree slope in the middle of the stairway on the flat strip. However this day as he turned he slammed straight into an elderly gentleman and rumble-tumbled him down the first flight of forty steps! Dam and the man ended up at the bottom of the stairs embracing Dam's bicycle somewhat intimately.

After that Dam spent quite a few weeks in horse-piddle as he called hospitals and the elderly gentleman went to horse-piddle too and had to be paid lots of money. Fred, as he was called, said he was an opal miner and Dam running into him was worth more to him than his fifty years spent opal mining! Dam had to save lots of money to pay for Fred's horse-piddleization. Dam had never seen an opal and was intrigued.

One day as Dam was working in the electrical shop wiring up radios a woman came in with an opal broach on her chest. Dam's transmission crackled and his radio-waves fizzed as his shoes began to smoulder. He kept watching the opal rise and fall above her breasts until he could contain himself no longer.

"Is that an opal?" he asked the lady.

"It's black fire," she said and added, "Don't look at it, it will send you mad!" Dam looked at it then looked at her and asked if it had had that effect on her.

She smiled and touched the voltmeter which Dam had in his hand. She didn't register any charge, she was dead.

"No earth," said Dam. The woman replied.

"You have to dig it young man, way down in de earth you'll find a blazing light." Dam's electric lips slid sideways and his mouth dropped open. He gazed into the fiery pendulum in front of him. "Under water it will shine," she said.

That night Dam dreamt he was digging in a lot of mud when a siren kept screaming in his ears. He woke up in a blinding flash of blue light just in time to jog across the bridge with his gas-mask on.

As the months went by he obtained books on opal mining and drew up plans for his departure from the city to the mines of Lightning Ridge. He figured that his thorough grounding in electronics would be of assistance to him. So after he saved a little extra money he went and visited Fred, the old gentleman he'd nearly killed on the Harbour Bridge.

Fred lived in an old person's home with a ramp instead of stairs down to it. Fred was in a wheel-chair and barely recognised Dam without his gas-mask on. Fred told lots of stories about the old days of opal mining and warned Dam to be wary of the gasses which could creep up behind you in the underground and rob one of good oxygen.

Fred said Dam would need a good generator. Dam said that was fine as he was attracted to electrical gadgetry. Fred went on; he would need a ladder and a good helmet and a strong back. Dam pushed Fred up the ramp into the sunlight.

"It's like living down a hole, this place" he said looking back down the ramp.

"There's one thing about opal mining which beats all other activities" he continued, "and that is the lure of finding a really good stone. Diamonds are diamonds and gold is gold but opals are treasures!" Dam could hardly wait.

He wanted to go then and there.

"But be prepared for the worst," said Fred. "If you don't find anything you'll end up with a bad back like me!" Dam turned the wheel chair to go down the ramp and unexpectedly it took off. Dam braced himself for the slide but Fred had his hand on the brake too suddenly for Dam who was catapulted right over Fred and crashed into the wall at the bottom of the ramp. Luckily for Dam he was stopped by an electrical box on the wall it read, 'Beware 10,000 volts!'

Dam, a little shocked rose up from the ground but Fred crashed into him squashing him into the electrical box again!

Dam was quite bruised as he hobbled up the ramp.

"Good luck" cried Fred, "You may need it!"

Now Dam being diligent raced home and began designing a ladder to put down the hole. Then he began to design a light system to illuminate the underground. He went and brought a pick and a shovel and a good strong helmet.

Dam left work the next day he was ready as he'd ever be. He went to a car auction place and bought a huge truck - next he bought a generator and a sleeping bag. Finally the great day came! He hung up his gas-mask and said farewell to the city he was bound for cleaner air.

He climbed up into his truck kicked the gears and turned the huge steering wheel. On the way out of the city he came upon ten red lights.

"Just my luck!" he said.

When he reached the freeway he suddenly remembered he'd left the stove on! But that wasn't all, he remembered what Fred had said about the toxic gasses down the mine and he'd forgotten his World War One gas-mask. The truck roared to a halt and did a U turn. On the way back home he encountered another ten red lights. When he arrived at his house the stove was on and a saucepan was red hot! There was something in it too which looked like his breakfast which he thought he had eaten. The air was bad so he put his gas-mask on and luckily he found his voltmeter on the table which he carried everywhere and he thought he'd put in the truck. Dam never went anywhere without his voltmeter.

He climbed up to the cabin of the truck which was like a giant empty water-tank on wheels and was soon roaring up the road issuing every conceivable sound.

"Damn!" said Dam as he came upon the first red light, "Oh no!" he said again as he came upon the second. At the third red light he noticed some road workers huddled around an electrical box. Dam being attracted to electricity reckoned they might need some help so he stopped the truck, hopped out and went over to see. When Dam stuck his head in amongst them and peered down at the electrical wires they all stood back very quickly as he'd forgotten to take his gas-mask off!

"Who the hell are you?" they all said.

"Voltmeter?" said Dam as he fumbled in his pocket. But with the gas-mask on the words sounded like 'hold Peter!' They saw him fumbling in his pocket and looked into his gas-mask eyes. The men looked at each other then back at Dam who withdrew the voltmeter from his pocket. One of the men thinking it was a bomb tackled poor Dam and wrestled him to the ground; another man grabbed the voltmeter and studied its dial. Dam took his gas-mask off.

"I was only trying to help!" he cried. Now as it so happened a voltmeter was exactly what they needed. They laughed and Dam stuck his head in amongst them again and wired up the voltmeter. It was just as they thought no earth. Dam had helped after all. He climbed back into his truck after getting his foot entangled in the gas-mask, said "green lights" to the men and was off. Dam was stopped by another seven red lights and when he finally reached the freeway he was booked by a policeman for speeding!

This time Dam was on his way. He passed town after town and spent two days driving. When he stopped for lunch it was on the second day. He staggered into a road house to buy some food but all they had was meat pies. Dam hated meat pies they gave him terrible wind. He spent the rest of the trip with his gas- mask on.

When he finally arrived at Lightning Ridge, he drove straight through it.

One hundred kilometres the other side he stopped his truck and looked at his map. The road just seemed to peter off into the desert! It was no good he'd have to ask somebody directions. The first person he found was another one hundred kilometres down the track, way out in the desert!

"Back that way to the little house on the corner" he was told. The road was incredibly bumpy and by the time he'd driven back two hundred kilometres it was dark and the truck ran out of fuel.

He looked around. He'd not seen a small house on a corner and the country side looked exactly the same as where he'd come from.

Dam slept in the cabin and dreamt there was a whole bunch of kangaroos with gas masks on having a party in the back of his truck. They were all dressed in road-traffic authority orange and thumped around till morning. Dam woke early and stepped outside on the frosty ground. Something made him look up underneath his truck and there jammed beneath the axle and the tray were twenty dead kangaroos.

Dam was horrified and spent all that day pulling them out and burying them in a large hole he dug with his pick and shovel. As he was digging the hole it started to rain and the kangaroos floated to the surface. Dam didn't know it but it was the first rain out there for twenty years! Fortunately he was on a slight hill so he dug a little drain to let the water out. It rained harder so he made the drain larger. Eventually he found he had to dig a great long trench to let the water out.

That took him the whole of the next day and the water didn't want to flow down his drain anyway! As he was filling in the hole he noticed one of the rocks looked odd so he put it in the cabin of the truck. Eventually the hole was filled and he climbed like a monkey back into the cabin. He was just about to try and start the engine when he remembered he'd run out of fuel.

He was on a hill so he thought he may be able to push the truck and roll some distance. He went to the rear and started pushing. He was only a little person and the truck would not move.

Dam decided he needed a lever so he began to look about for a stick. He saw one some distance off so he set off in that direction. That stick was no good and he saw another several hundred meters away. That one was no good either.

He spied another way off in the distance and after he reached it and turned to go back he saw that the truck was over a kilometre away!

The stick broke. Dam said damn as he sat down with a huff but he shot into the air again as he'd sat on a bunch of prickles. Dam ended up having to jack the back of the truck up and make two little ramps for the two back wheels to run down when he let the jack down. After sometime the truck was half a metre in the air so he let the jack down quickly.

The truck took off at a great pace with Dam running along behind in a cloud of dust. Gradually he came along side and tried to grip the door handle and leap up. But the truck began to go faster! Two kilometres down the road it slowed then stopped. Dam raced up to it and jumped in to the cabin where he feverishly gripped the wheel. He stayed there a while puffing and panting. Then slowly very slowly it started to roll back the other way! Dam gripped the wheel and stared into the rear vision mirror.

"At least it's moving" he said to himself as he rolled back a kilometre.

The sun blazed down and he felt hungry and thirsty. Knowing that he must stay with his vehicle he sat down and waited for a car. Two days later the first car came along and Dam hailed it down. It was an American or a 'Merry-can' as Dam called them and his wife on a tour around 'Horse-trailer' which was Dam's word for Australia. He asked them if they knew where Lightning Ridge was and they said they'd never heard of it. As they drove off Dam noticed his jack in the back of their car! He was just about to call out when the car took off at high speed.

Dam sat down on the road, he was feeling a little miserable and he hadn't eaten in days. He decided to take a little walk and set off up the next hill. By the time he reached the top his shoes were full of prickles and he was six inches taller. His tongue was hanging out and his eyes were full of dust. He peered over the edge of the slope. Way off in the distance beyond a slight bend was a house and a shed, so he went back to his truck and found some money for petrol.

He took a short cut through the countryside and by the time he came close to the house he was ten inches taller with all the prickles stuck to his shoes.

He noticed somebody walk from the house to the shed so Dam went around the back to find them. He looked in the shed but nobody was there. He noticed the back door was open so he went around the back of the shed but nobody was there. He went back around to the front but nobody was there. He heard a noise on the other side of the shed so he went around there, still nobody. He sat down to get the prickles out of his shoes. While he was sitting there he noticed a man walking backwards towards him.

"Hello," said Dam. Well the man got such a shock he leapt into the air.

He seemed to jump a lot faster than he talked!

"Oh petrol?" he said very slowly - was ten kilometres that way. Dam set off he'd soon be in Lightning Ridge and he thought he might be able to get a taxi back out to his truck. By the time he arrived he was another ten inches taller. The town was full of weird looking short people with long frizzy hair and beards the colour of the dust. It was only when he cleaned his shoes that he realised he was about the same size.

Dam borrowed a petrol tin from the garage and inquired about taxis.

"Yes there's one behind the garage you can borrow," said the man. The taxi turned out to be a rickety old bicycle. Dam thanked the man and peddled off after a lunch of meat pies. When Dam reached his truck he found it had a flat tyre. It took him ages to change it as he did not have a jack and had to dig a big hole in the road. He also spent more time in the bushes than he wanted to.

He realised now why the townsfolk looked like the colour of the road, it was all the meat pies they ate! Every time he leant on the wheel-brace to undo or do up a nut he had to go lightning fast back to the bushes.

"I guess that's why they call it Lightning Ridge" he said.

Dam rolled into town and returned the deluxe taxi to the garage. As he was talking to the man Dam remembered the odd rock he'd found whilst burying the kangaroos. He reached in the cabin and pulled it out. It turned out to be a 'knobby' as he called it and Dam was advised to crack it open as opal came in such stones.

"Opal!" said Dam and he had visions of digging up all the kangaroos. "Opal!" he said again and went over to his truck to look for his pick but Dam being diligent had left it back at the kangaroos. He thanked the garage attendant again and took off at full speed back to his little Lightning Ridge.

Fortunately the pick and shovel were still there. The flat tyre as well which he'd forgotten to put in the truck.

Dam grabbed the pick and smashed the stone with a single blow, colour exploded everywhere!

"Opal!" he cried as he began to pick up the pieces. He threw everything in the back of the truck and took off for town. He went straight to the mining office and asked to stake a claim.

"Back down the road." He found however that it was not that simple. He had to buy a compass and a tape measure and a new type of map. He bought lots of meat pies and other food and filled his containers with bore water. The bore water tasted as ghastly as the meat pies. He was horrified when it came out of a tap. He'd heard about the bores and how people used to hunt them with dogs. The garage attendant said it was fine to drink. Dam couldn't imagine how they could collect so much of it. Maybe it had something to do with the bore bathes; he couldn't work it out. Over time he grew kind of used to it; it was the only thing to wash the meat pies down with. At first the chemical combination was phenomenal and he was glad he lived alone!

Dam drove off, he'd become an opal miner. The opal he'd found was gem quality but he'd smashed it to smithereens and it was worthless. Everybody asked where he found it and Dam only said that the kangaroos found it.

Dam set up camp next to his favourite kangaroos and for the next couple of weeks spent most of his time on his hands and knees studying each pebble.

Strangely each one seemed to flash colour at him and he'd pick it up in a great hurry only to find it was an ordinary stone. He devised hand and knee pads to stop the prickles spearing him and more than once he'd forgotten about them and sat down, his bottom acting like a pin-cushion.

At night Dam would lie back to look at the opalised stars. He thought about the Harbour Bridge and his city job and realised that he was alone in the big world no matter where he was. Somehow he felt contented out there surrounded by prickles and dust. Of course he was sure there were millions of dollars in opals right underneath his bed. Opals as large as footballs.

Dam learnt that opal occurs eighty meters under the ground or was it eighty feet? It didn't seem to matter so long as it was there. He also knew that most miners used diving rods to locate underground faults in the sandstone where there was a good chance of coming across a pocket of knobbies. Then Dam had a plan.

Next day he made a diving rod out of a piece of wire and spent many hours going round and around. That was no good so he fetched the battery from the truck and connected it to his pick which he drove into the ground. He pulled his voltmeter out of his pocket and connected it to an intricate wiring system he'd made from an old fence. This array included his truck and several dinner plates and knives and forks which he'd stuck in the ground. Next he found a huge rock which he dropt on the ground in various places and studied the dial on the voltmeter. His theory was that dense patches beneath the soil would carry electrical impulses quicker and that with all his knives and forks and plates sticking in the dirt and bits of wire hanging out like hair on a scalp, one of the 'receivers' was sure to send an impulse to the voltmeter.

Nothing happened so he turned the dial on the voltmeter to millivolts, still nothing happened. Then he suddenly received a hell of a shock as he dropt the rock on his foot. Out of scientific necessity he searched out his last orange and stuck the rusty negative earth wire into it. Still nothing happened.

Dam spent the rest of the day tripping over wire and getting hopelessly entangled. At one stage he accidentally shorted out the battery and he felt sure his hair stood on end!

There was nothing else to do but to dig amongst the rotten kangaroos with his gas-mask on. He spent the next day digging another hole for them and carried each one over to the hole and when each one had been buried for a second time he went back to the old hole and started to dig.

Day and night he dug. During the hot day and by the light of the silvery moon. Down and down he went studying each rock. By the end of four weeks he was down three metres.

"Only another seventy one metres to go!" he said.

On one of his fortnightly trips into town he was talking to the garage attendant who advised him to hire a drilling rig to dig the hole. Well it would save a bit of time thought Dam who was digging through sandstone.

The day the drilling rig came it was raining slightly and the ground seemed alive with colour, fresh and clean.

"Eighty meters!" the man said, "You've got to be joking!"

"Oh?" said Dam, "Yes…he was."

"Eighty feet at the most!" said the driller.

Dam was relieved and excited that that very afternoon he was going to be rich! Rich! Rich! When the machine was through the sandstone and began to pull up opal dirt which is clay, the man switched off his machine and studied the dirt.

"You might have something here," he said picking up a large knobby.

Dam grabbed it and put it in his voltmeter pocket, paid the man and said goodbye. Dam peered down into his hole it was cold and black and deep.

How was he going to climb down there? The knobby the driller man had found turned out to be black potch which is opal rock without colour, a good sign.

Next day he went into town to buy some rope and organise a ladder.

He bought a whole lot of iron and a welding kit. He spent weeks welding up the various sections of the ladder. He used the rope to lower the sections of ladder down the hole and a windlass to haul the buckets of dirt up from the bottom.

Dam's ladder was ready and he used his truck to back the pieces up to the hole and lower them down as they were so heavy. He would then climb down the hole with his gas-mask on and his helmet and tie the pieces of ladder together. When Dam reached the bottom he looked around, nothing. He dug into the wall a little and a knobby fell out and hit his foot and then another.

He had a candle mounted on top of his helmet. He picked the knobbies up and climbed back up.

He chipped away at their edges. No colour only black potch. A disappointed Dam climbed into his truck and drove twenty meters back to camp but alas when he stopped the truck he realised the rope was still attached to the bottom of the ladder and he'd bent and jammed the ladder in the hole! He peered into the hole and it was full of bent and tested metal.

Dam being diligent undid the rope and attached a smaller section of it to the top of the ladder. He revved the truck and took off at high speed and the ladder sprang out like a spring and flew in front of the truck where it seemed to possess a life of its own and danced about for a while before coming to rest in a mangled heap. Dam spent weeks heating it up and straightening it out.

One day he noticed some people watching him from some distance away.

He raised his hat and kept welding. Next day two more people arrived and walked around and around. Then almost overnight caravans and tents, trucks and generators, cars and people were thick in the bushes about him. What was going on? He went over to ask someone who said there was a Russian.

Now Dam wasn't racist. He didn't mind what race one belonged to.

He thought there were Chinese people in town and he'd seen a few Japanese - he didn't mind foreigners at all. He couldn't imagine so many people avoiding a Russian. He went back to his camp and watched their activities, he was somewhat confused.

Pretty soon the drilling rig arrived and holes were going down everywhere and people began bringing their mining machinery in. Some had mechanical hoists for pulling buckets of dirt up from down below and others had great big 'blowers' which were huge vacuum cleaners which sucked the dirt up from eighty feet down and deposited it in trucks.

The trucks would then rumble off to the puddling dams where the opal dirt was mixed with water and the knobbiest and potch washed clean. Dam looked on intrigued. His nights were electrified by the cackle of generators and electric lights, cars came and went at all hours. His opalescent stars seemed an awfully long way away. Maybe if he pretended to be a Russian he'd scare them all off.

There were obviously some rich people mining. Their huge machines squashed trees and made mountains of dirt. Then the cry went up that good opal was indeed beneath the surface and Dam heard faint rumours that he was surrounded by wealthy claims.

Dam's ladder was finished and he spent a day fitting it all together down the hole. He was ready to load his first bucket. He had a rope going up to his windlass which he wound up by hand. A little primitive but it worked.

He ventured into town to purchase some supplies and received quite a fright when he looked at himself in the rear vision mirror of his truck. His hair was long and frizzy he had an opal miner's beard which was the colour of the dust and his teeth looked like dinosaur fossils. His eyes were full of mud, he stank like a forgotten bag of groceries and he hadn't even started mining yet!

The garage attendant told him some big stones were coming out of a place called 'Dam's Rush.' Dam wondered if it had anything to do with him.

On his way back to camp he noticed a sign which read 'cockatiels for sale.'

He stopped the truck and went inside. The lady said the birds were good mining companions and could talk. Many miners used them to warn them if the air was not good down the mine.

So Dam bought a baby one and put it on his shoulder. It immediately started biting Dam's ear and pulling his hair out. He called it 'Lucky' and even taught it to say its own name but soon stopped as the bird couldn't pronounce the 'L' correctly and it sounded more like 'f..k me!'

Dam climbed down his hole with Lucky on his shoulder and a candle on top of his helmet. With his gas-mask and the mining pick and shovel and for some reason he still had his voltmeter in his pocket.

Dam began to dig and fill the bucket which he'd lowered before. He hauled up one bucket after another, his back felt like chewing gum and his muscles grew like fungal growths. After a week of furious mining he flopped down in his prickle proof hammock and slept for two days. He woke in the night feeling refreshed and resumed mining.

Way down in the hole the air was cool and pleasant. It was black down there anyway, permanent night. Dam worked with candles as he found he didn't need the bright light of the generator and it chewed up a lot of fuel. He was quite happy picking away, it kept him healthy and he had his bird to talk to.

It took him one week to fill the truck which was pretty fast going and he set off to the puddling dam with his first load of dirt. He could barely contain his excitement as he tipped it into the puddler which he hired for the occasion.

Dam's eyes watched the dirt being churned around and around. There seemed to be a bucket full of knobbies in the basket. He went back to his camp and spent the rest of the day snipping them open. At last he found some colour. It was only small but it was colour. Looking into it he perfused himself into opal and dreamt of opal flashes for days.

Dam was exalted now and he began to dig more furiously for opal fever was upon him. Bucket after bucket flew up the mine shaft and in one day the truck was full. Early the next morning he was off to the puddling dam again.

He revved the engine which was slow to start and took off at high speed.

The truck was sluggish however as the carburettor needed cleaning. This was a happy day for Dam and he passed some people who waved and grinned as much as he. He put the truck into high gear and kept the revvs up. At the dam he noticed a strange contraption on the road behind him. As he moved it moved! Then he saw his rope and recognised his ladder. He'd pulled the ladder out of the hole again!

"Not to worry there's a million dollars in this load" he said backing up to the puddler. He tipped the truck and ran around and watched it all being washed. Once again there were lots of knobbies in the load. As Dam watched he became quite giddy and actually fell in the puddler! He was flying round and round several times before being spat out at tremendous speed. Fortunately he landed in the mud and went right under. When he emerged he couldn't see a thing and gave his head a wack on the back of the tail-gate of his truck. He washed his face and tried to turn the puddler off but couldn't. The kill switch was jammed and he could hear his stones rumbling into tiny bits. He dared not look in the puddler again. He'd heard about stones being smashed in puddlers.

Dam suddenly raced away from the puddler looking for a stick to jam in the cogs. He ran this way and that like a startled ant but there weren't any sticks for miles. He ran back to the puddler and took off one of his boots and squashed it in the cogs which merrily chewed it up and kept going round and around!

He took off his other boot off and jammed that in too. The machine made a complete mess of that boot too! Then out of desperation he tore the front seat out of the truck and jammed that in the cogs. That stopped it!

With the machine making an agonizing noise he climbed into the basket and filled his bucket with the knobbies. He wound up his rope and hoisted the mangled ladder as best he could onto the back of the truck and hurried back to camp. He left his shoes and the car seat jammed in the puddler so he drove the truck half standing; quite a feat!

Back at camp he jumped down out of his truck straight onto lots of prickles.

After extracting these he cautiously tip-toed to a safe place where he could snip his knobbies.

More colour! He was overjoyed. Opal shimmers shot across the sky, even his fingernails had opals underneath them. He threw his rope down the hole and barefoot climbed down it. It was midnight and Dam was singing down his hole and Lucky was joining in. When the bucket was full he grabbed the rope and began to climb up it. But the more he pulled the more the rope gave way then suddenly all the rope came flying down the hole!

The bird ducked for cover and Dam dodged to the side. His candle went out. It was black. He could see the opalescent stars winking at him way up above.

He lit his candle and looked down at the rope. Some idiot hadn't tied it on properly at the other end! Somehow he was going to have to crawl out of the hole as nobody would know he was there and nobody would hear him.

He didn't want to spend the night sleeping in opal dirt nor did he want to dig anymore. Dam bit his bottom lip; it was going to be a tough climb to say the least!

Dam lay horizontally on the ground and stretched himself out with his feet touching one side of the hole and his shoulders touching the other. His head was bent up. He tried many positions and that was the only way and the most comfortable. Inch by painful inch he watched his bare feet crawl up the other wall followed by a wiggle of his shoulders. With the candle and the bird on his stomach, slowly, very slowly he wriggled upwards. After about three hours he reckoned he was half way up. The candle had gone out long ago, at last after dripping hot wax all over his stomach. The poor terrified bird had walked onto Dam's nose where it dug its claws in and gripped it like a branch.

Dam was hissing and spitting. His shoulders felt like angle iron and his dimly lit delicate electronic toes looked horribly normal. His arms were splayed out below him, his fingers inched along the wall of the hole digging in to the smallest groove or hanging onto the sandstone by the texture of skin alone.

When he reached the top sometime around dawn, his whole body felt like a piece of steel, cold and rigid. At the surface he hesitated not knowing what to do. So far so good now came the difficult part. How was he going to spin around and grasp the outside of the hole? Lucky, the bird, walked up his forehead and sprang onto flat ground. It soon turned around and began to help pulling Dam up by tearing out his hair. Then Dam remembered the legs of the windlass and with a mammoth effort he spun around and caught one of its legs.

He hung there gasping for air, his legs dangling in the black hole and his head locked onto the edge, his nose acting like a tin opener, held him aloft.

With another huge effort he swung a leg up and out then the rest of his body followed. He lay there on his back still staring straight at his feet with the early dawn shimmering above him. He lay there a long time.

Dam had a very bad kink in his neck. In fact he couldn't take his eyes off his feet for weeks. His back was rigid and his chin seemed to be stuck to his chest. He could only just stand and as he shuffled about his camp looking down he noticed the ground an awful lot more.

The day finally arrived when he had to drive his truck into town and Dam being diligent had improvised a strong cardboard box to use as a seat.

The whole process was extremely difficult for him though, as he had to use a mirror tied around his neck to see out the windscreen because he couldn't lift his head quite high enough! This meant that everything appeared upside down so he drove very slowly.

When he was on the main road going along quite well with no warning at all the box gave way and for a moment trapped him with his head between his knees. It was very difficult holding the wheel however he did manage to turn the ignition key off. He had absolutely no hope of finding the brake. The bird didn't know where to sit for a while and only when the truck slowed to a crawl did it stop saying its rude name! Dam's legs were stuck up in the air for an awfully long time. He heard a number of vehicles pass by, none of them stopped. The only way he could get out of the box was to open the door and drop to the ground. Unfortunately for Dam the box hit the ground before he did which made his arms stick up in the air much like his feet and forced him into the box more!

There he sat in the middle of the road a box with two legs and two arms sticking out of it. He tried to call for help but his nose was flat up against the mirror and a small grunt was all that came out. Then he felt the bird land on his bare feet where it began to nibble his toes. The real problem however was the noise of an approaching truck. Dam didn't know where he was in relation to the oncoming traffic and as the noise got louder he began to pray to God and with his hands and feet pointing skyward he figured he was in the right position!

He began to wiggle his fingers and wave his toes frantically and utter loud grunting sounds. The truck however slowed down and came to a halt five feet from the box.

"Hey come and have a look at this!" he heard one voice say "This is the first packaged road-kill I've ever seen."

"It might be alive!" said another voice. Dam grunted profusely. They lay him on his side and pulled the box off. Dam emerged like an unfolding flower.

He thanked the men still looking down into his mirror.

The men said 'Merry Christmas!' and took off down the road. Dam climbed back up into the cabin and was soon on his way again doing a kind of accelerator-mirror shuffle.

"What happened to you?" said the garage attendant. And Dam told him he had to climb out of his hole.

"Holy hell!" is all the attendant could say and added, "You need a dip in the bore baths!"

Dam drove off to the bore baths and found several foreigners gathered about the edge.

"What happened to you?" they asked as Dam shuffled out of the change rooms his mirror in hand to see where he was walking. Dam said nothing he was in pain. He could hear them say, "Looks like he climbed out of a hole!"

Dam tried grinning and smiling but they couldn't see his dinosaur teeth.

He hoped they wouldn't think he was a Russian.

The hot bore water stank and he wondered how they kept it so hot.

Dam gently lowered himself in and put his head under. His toes sparkled as they went lobster pink. Slowly very slowly he could hear his bones crunching as he tried to move. They were jammed together with opal dust and the powder was dry like the desert or ground up potch and he felt a little relieved.

He went back to his camp and lay down with his mirror on his chest and watched the stars. Would he ever descend into his hole again! He could bend his knees a little better but his neck was still as stiff as a brake pedal.

Dam drove each day to the bore baths and each day immersed himself in its sulphurous depths. Then one day as he was studying his feet in the green algal gloom somebody said they had a good opal. Dam looked up and as he did there was a mighty crack as his neck went back into place.

"Oh!" cried Dam, "my neck!" Everybody looked at him but they were more absorbed looking at the opal. Dam jumped out of the water to have a look. Miraculously he was cured. He just caught a glimpse of the stone as it was put away though he could have looked at it for ages as it was a good one.

Dam learnt that it had come from a place called "Dam's Rush." He recognised the person who had the stone; it was the lady from next to his camp. Dam was bemused to think that a rush could be named after him when he'd never even found a stone! He stretched his neck like a tortoise and smiled.

That afternoon he studied his ladder to see if it was repairable. Some of it was but it had already been repaired once and he thought it wiser to buy new pieces of steel and make a new one. So the next day he set about making a new ladder. The old one he made into walls of a new room which he extended onto his camp. It was looking quite civilised.

It was just as well he made it for as soon as it was finished it started to rain.

A storm brewed and thunder rolled about the countryside. Lightning was coming ever nearer and Dam being fearful of it put his new boots on.

He'd heard that if one had rubber soles on, the lightning would not strike you. He crawled into his hammock with his boots on and hid under the pillow.

The bird slept under his chin. It rained and it poured for three days solid.

All the roads turned into dangerous mud puddles and the mud stuck to one's shoes until one was carrying wheelbarrows of mud around and one couldn't move.

While it was raining Dam acquainted himself with the lady next door and she said that her husband had found the stone right on their adjoining border.

Dam had a good look at the stone and was beginning to see flashes of colour in his mind again. All that night opal auroras caressed and fluoresced across his dreams. The next morning he was devising plans again and by lunch time he began to assemble his new ladder. One week later he went down his hole again and was just about to tie on the last piece of ladder when his feet touched water.

His mine had ten feet of water in it!

Dam being diligent was unperturbed and went back up top and started his generator. He fetched his gas-mask and lowered his water-proofed light down the hole. Holding the light in one hand he dived down and found the bucket and hitched a rope to it. As he was doing so he opened his eyes close to the wall and to his surprise noticed they were covered in knobbies. They were all so easy to see! Remembering what the woman in the shop long ago had said about water and opal Dam did a little exploring. It was as she had said.

"Put a little water on it and it will shine!" Dam shot back up the ladder and hauled the bucket up. That night as he lay awake, he devised a novel method for mining underwater.

Next day he drove into town and bought all the necessary apparati for his venture. He was also growing quite used to meat pies and bought a great stack of them. He bought a new metal bucket and lots of pipe. He bought an air compressor and his friend gave him lots of old car tyre inner-tubes.

As soon as he was back at camp he set about implementing his ideas. He cut a window in the side of the bucket. He put the pipe onto his air compressor and attached the other end to the gas mask. Then he cut the inner tubes into small lengths and slipped them over his arms and legs like a kind of wet-suit.

He ate six meat pies and washed them down with bore water.

He was ready. He lowered his pick down the hole in his knobby bucket.

He put Lucky on his shoulder under the bucket which captured some air.

The bird immediately started nibbling Dam's ear which Dam found immensely irritating. He tied the bucket down so it wouldn't float off. Dam really was going underwater opal mining!

He started the generator and the air fizzed into the gas-mask. This time Dam was sure he was going to find an opal. As he climbed down the ladder the bucket on his head was heavy and he hoped his neck would not go out again as he'd forgotten his mirror and he would not be able to see where he was going! He made sure he hadn't forgotten anything else though for he had overalls on under the inner-tubes and he'd even remembered to bring his voltmeter!

The cold water sizzled in between the inner-tubes and his flesh. Pretty soon he was on the bottom but the air in the upturned bucket kept him afloat. Fortunately he was able to fill his pockets with nobbies which weighed him down and enabled him to walk around normally.

Suddenly Dam began to feel a little ill with pains in his stomach again! Whether it was the extra pressure of being underwater eighty feet down a hole or perhaps he was a victim of the meat pies? Then all hell broke loose and Lucky started screaming its name in his ear! The noise was unbearable and Dam tried talking to it to tell it to be quiet. Then he started shouting inside the bucket which only made things worse! Suddenly the bird fell on its side! It was dead! "Toxic gasses!" yelled Dam and made a dash for the ladder. As he was half running, half swimming he saw a beam of bright colour gleam from the wall. "Opal!" he cried trying to hold his breath. He took his pick and struck at it but on the second strike accidentally smashed the light bulb. Great blue flames darted about in the water and he could feel his voltmeter leaping about in his pocket. That's all he remembered as he blacked out.

When he came to, after he doesn't know how long, he found himself floating on top of the water at the bottom of his hole. The only reason he wasn't drowned was because his neck had gone out again and his nose was just above water level. Slowly, very slowly, he dragged himself up the ladder and out of the hole. His pockets were still full of nobbies and his excitement rose as he neared the surface.

When he reached daylight he found his bird was on top of his helmet!

Dam still can't explain how it got there. It was alright and started singing in the sunshine when it reached the fresh air.

Dam dragged himself over to his chair and sat down but the weight of him broke the chair. He lay on the floor feeling totally rubberised. Gradually he emptied his pockets of nobbies and took the inner-tubes off his limbs. He lay there for some time soaking up the warmth and staring at his feet again.

That was it! He'd had enough! He was going back to the city! As he sat on the floor snipping his knobbies and each one of them was either black or grey with no colour, he said again that he wasn't going back down that hole!

He decided to sell his truck as a first step and buy a normal car.

The next day with his mirror round his neck he climbed into the cabin of his truck and tried to start it but it would not go. He tried again and again until the battery was flat. He knew that at least. He didn't need his voltmeter to tell him that, besides it had been electrocuted into oblivion. He nearly killed his bird, his neck was out again and he'd squashed his only chair and found nothing, nothing!

He'd have to hitch a ride into town, go to the bore baths, buy a new battery and hitch back again.

With his head down looking at the mirror which guided his path, he and Lucky set off shuffling along the road. Nobody stopped, several cars passed but they must have thought he looked rather odd. He began to kick stones and one particular round one rolled along and bumped into a larger one and split open. In the mirror a little way off Dam caught the sight of a vivid red flash.

He dashed forward and picked it up.

There in his hand was two halves of an electric red on black stone. It was gem quality and was worth hundreds of thousands of dollars!

The very next car picked him up. He was standing in the middle of the road waving his arms around like a lunatic flashing his stones.

His neck seemed suddenly alright as he got in the car. It was the Merry-can and his wife still on a tour around 'Horse-trailer.' They asked Dam if he knew where Lightning Ridge was and if that was where he'd found the stone.

Dam looked beside him on the seat and saw his old truck jack lying on the floor.

Lucky began to answer all their questions with many expletives. All Dam could do was shed tears of joy.

19

Dam Goes Bushwalking

Dam lived all alone. He was beginning to talk to himself in his reflection in the dishwater. Once he had found himself in the washing machine and often sang to himself in the bath. But that was not enough. He needed some company, someone to talk to. So he joined a bush-walking club and decided to meet some new faces and talk politics to someone besides himself.

Dam found some bush-walking groups in the telephone book but then decided he'd prefer to go bird watching instead so he rang a bird watchers club. Dam loved birds, he often spoke in their language and could call owls and eagles and get them to come in quite close.

Years ago Dam had a pet cat which he loved. He'd kept it for many years and knew that it too was fond of birds! Poor Dam the first day he found 'Tiddles' with a dead bird he was furious. Dam being diligent cooked the bird in garlic and fed it to Tiddles. The cat never killed another bird! When Tiddles died Dam made a funny hat out of Tiddles coat. The hat hung down over Dam's head with poor Tiddles paws either side of Dam's ears.

The day Dam was going bird watching was very cold and windy, he had already decided to wear Tiddles so he pulled her down over his ears and set off.

Some distance away near the forest a sighting of a rare Screech Owl had been recorded so the other bird watchers were delighted to have Dam come along though they didn't know he could make Screech Owl calls. The plan was to meet before night then walk along the well-made trail for an hour or so and come back in the dark. It sounded like fun to Dam who'd been wearing dark glasses for days and nights to prepare his eyes for seeing in the dark.

Dam arrived in his little blue car with his dark glasses on and Tiddles lashed to his head. When he took his dark glasses off he was blinded and could not see more than ten feet in front. Dam shook hands with everybody and introduced Tiddles.

"Oh he looks so nice!" said one lady.

"It's a she," said Dam.

"Oh, I've never seen a green cat before!" said the lady.

"Nor had I until I fed her garlic!" said Dam who was rolling his huge torch around in his pocket. This was splendid, he was enjoying himself.

"SSSHHH!" said the leader. Dam jumped, he thought there was a snake close by. Then she said, "Everybody quiet!" That was all she seemed to say the whole night! Dam's bottom lip came out and he looked disgruntled, all he wanted to do was talk. He walked at the end of the line looking at the ground. The forest was tall and dark. Dam couldn't see a thing until he took his glasses off.

"What's that?" squeaked a lady. Dam crashed into the back of her and she crashed into the person in front who was only just saved by the person in front of her.

"Oh sorry!" said Dam out loud.

"SSHHH!" said everybody.

Dam thought damn and they kept walking. They had come a fair distance along the track and had not seen or heard any owls only the cry of a few lonely swans migrating overhead. They kept walking. People were occasionally flashing their torches around then turning them off. Dam had a plan.

All of a sudden, with no warning at all, Dam let out a terrific Screech Owl call! For those of you who do not know what a Screech Owl sounds like, it sounds like a terrified screaming woman. The line of people in front fell in a heap of writhing bodies on the track.

"Oh I am sorry!" said Dam.

There were loud exclamations and torches flashing everywhere.

"Did you see it?" they said.

"Yes!" said Dam. "It was really close."

"It flew over that way," he said pointing to some trees and added, "I'll go in and see if I can flush it out!"

"Oh, let me come too" said the woman who had admired Tiddles.

"It might be dangerous!" said Dam.

"Nonsense," she said.

The others waited on the track and Dam and the lady tiptoed off into the bushes. They had not gone far when Dam let out another shriek. Dam swears he saw the woman's hat lift four inches in the air!

The forest was pitch black and they continued on with torches flashing everywhere. It wasn't Dam's fault that his torch was the largest of everybody else's. He flashed it in the ladies eyes so much she went totally blind. All she could see when the torch was taken away was a large white spot! But then Dam's torch suddenly went dead. He couldn't believe it and then he too couldn't see anything. Slowly his eyes became more accustomed to the light.

Then suddenly he stopped dead. There out the corner of his eyes was a massively huge gorilla! Dam was sure his hat rose six inches in the air! It was standing far above him silently watching. Then much to Dam's horror, as he turned to run something extremely strong grabbed him by the leg!

He leapt in the air squealing. But it gripped his leg with its strong teeth!

"Ahrrgh! Ahrrgh!" he cried desperately. He could see a faint torch light coming quickly his way through the trees then something stung his foot really badly!

He began pulling his leg furiously but his foot was stuck!

"Arrgh!" he yelled again as the woman flashed the torch in his eyes which absolutely blinded him. "There's a gorilla over there!" he whimpered pointing in the direction. The woman looked with the torch and saw an old tree stump.

Dam yelled "I'm stuck in a hole!"

"What sort of a hole" asked the lady.

"It's a foot hole," said Dam, "And it's about a foot long!"

"Can't you get it out!" said the lady. The others back on the track could hear Dam struggling and they called out,

"Are you alright!" The lady yelled back,

"He's about a foot long and he can't get it out!"

From back on the track came gasps and stunned silence as Dam cried,

"Arrgh!" again. He yanked and pulled and pulled and twisted. His foot was very stuck!

"Ahrrgh!" he yelled in despair, "Somethin's biting me!" With that the woman grabbed Dam's leg and pulled so hard he thought his foot would break off.

She didn't look like she has muscles like a gorilla.

"I'll get help," she said. "You wait here."

She left him in the dark, all alone with his foot stuck in a hole. He watched her go through the trees, her small light like a small firefly disappearing.

Dam could hear her crashing around for some time. The night was cold and the air crisp.

Suddenly he heard the flutter of giant wings then an ear-piercing scream like that of a screaming woman. Dam knew it was the Screech Owl so he called to it but there was silence… Dam waited and waited.

He was flicking his torch switch on and off and felt the hole around his ankle. Whatever it was that had bitten him was not biting any more. Maybe his foot was going numb and he couldn't feel it? Maybe it would swell and he'd never get it out! Perhaps, he thought, he may be dead in fifteen minutes from all the poison!

Dam waited and waited. One hour passed then two, then three. He was just about to lie down as best he could when something wacked him on the head really hard and began to lift Tiddles up! Whatever it was was so strong it pulled Dam's foot clean out of the hole!

It was the owl! It had attacked Tiddles and rescued Dam from the hole. Dam bent down to find his shoe.

"Thank you owl and thank you Tiddles," he said patting his head.

Dam looked up beyond the dark branches of the trees and into the stars.

They were casting enough light to see by and Dam's eyes were used to the dark. He meandered back to the track. In the trees above he could hear a small whispering sound. He knew it was the owl. Dam whispered back and the bird replied.

Dam couldn't see or hear any sign of the other people. He decided to go back to his car. He found the other people's cars were still there too.

Dam was feeling very hungry and thought that since they didn't come to rescue him they must have continued walking. Dam was limping a bit and he thought he'd better get along home to see if he hadn't been bitten by anything nasty.

Once at home he put his foot in a bucket of hot water. It had a lump on it as though he had been bitten by an ant. He had some dinner and thought nothing more about it. He was soon tucked in his own little bed fast asleep.

Several days later Dam happened to be listening to the radio when he heard that a bush-walker was still lost. He'd last been seen with his foot stuck in a hole and fear was held for his safety! The other bush-walkers had been found by search parties after spending two freezing nights and a day lost in the bush!

Dam rang the police.

"Hello, I was the one who was stuck in a hole!" he said.

"What kind of a hole?" asked the officer.

Dam rang the bird watchers club and said he was the one who was stuck in a hole. They too asked about the hole. Dam was intrigued that they should all want to know about the hole and didn't seem interested in him! They didn't seem interested in the Screech Owl either, so Dam said this,

"The hole was in the ground and my foot found it. My shoe got stock in it too and something bit my foot. The hole was a foot deep and my foot fitted exactly. The dirt was too hard to dig around in order to free my foot so I was stuck in the hole for about three hours. It wasn't a very pleasant hole; I've been in worse holes." Then Dam asked,

"Have you ever been stuck in a hole?"

Strange, thought Dam as the person hung up - nobody seemed interested in the Screech Owl!

20

Dam Goes Pig Hunting

To some people Dam was a bit of a bore. He just sat around and read books. The only thing that interested him and kept others slightly interested in him was that he collected dog poo to make book covers out of. He would put it in buckets of water first and use the watery waste to sprinkle on his lawn and around his fruit trees. The best books of course received the best hard covers and the drying and book press apparatus he used to bind the books with was entirely his own invention. Dam would then sell the books to an agent who would distribute them to bookstores often embossed in gold, odourless and waterproof.

Dam was proud of his book covering business and proud of his scientific experiments which were improving the durability of his product. He had tried all sorts of materials and had found the consistency of dog poo far surpassed anything else. That was until he went to the zoo and collected a little bag of pig manure from the pig pen.

He took it home and tried a few experiments on it. After drying it in the sun then adding this and that he produced a product which seemed to have considerable potential. But to carry out his experiments further he needed more manure.

Next day he came back with a whole bucket full of pig manure and set about boiling it and curing it in his kitchen. There he made some book covers and baked them in the oven like biscuits. They came out as hard as rocks and seemed to bind better and be more durable than the dog poo ones.

Dam then and there decided he needed lots of pigs to produce the superior book covers and to do that he was going to need to start a piggery.

There were lots of wild pigs in the outback, great black hairy ones.

He decided to take a holiday and drive out to where he could find a male and a few female pigs to bring home and keep in his orchard. He packed his little blue car and put in lots of cobs of corn as enticement for the pigs. For Dam had improvised a trap which was going to catch a couple of wild boars.

The trap consisted of a huge landing net with a long handle. This was suspended above the ground and the corn was placed beneath it with a trigger stick holding up the net. This stick was released by pulling on a long string.

Dam drove for half a day and set up camp in a patch of scrub. There were plenty of pigs around, he could smell them. He'd placed the corn under the net some distance away. Dam sat in his tree holding the trigger string. The night was clear and crisp. The ground had been dug up extensively and here and there were huge piles of black mud which made walking a little difficult.

It wasn't long before he heard strange noises. He sniffed the air then all of a sudden a hoard of wild boar came about his tree. There were dozens of them! Dam became so excited he nearly fell out of his tree. All he could see was book covers galore. The pigs were grunting and squealing and digging in the ground about. They bumped into the tree and it shook. Dam hung on and climbed a little higher. Some of the pigs had huge tusks and looked fearsome, some had piglets which ran about squealing.

Underneath the net a large number had gathered to eat the corn, the ground was completely black with them. There were so many Dam didn't need to pull the string, the stick was dislodged and the net came down. Great commotion broke out amongst the herd and those pigs that weren't in the net disappeared. The net was alive, it was leaping this way and that, bouncing up in the air and terrible noises were coming from it!

Dam leapt out of the tree, tripped and fell in a pile of mud. He was black. Undeterred he raced over to the net and grabbed the handle. The pigs took off as best they could in the opposite direction. Dam hung on to the handle slipping and sliding but they pulled him along and slowly gathered speed. He couldn't hold them still and soon he was breaking out into a run. Over mud and ditches he ran still holding his net full of pigs.

"Think of all the book covers I'll make with these!" he thought as he sped over the ground. The going was difficult, the ground was becoming muddier. Then he fell and was dragged some distance, but he still hung on. Now up and running fast again. Presently his tent flashed past and his car. They had run around in a big circle! He wondered how it was going to end.

Up a slight hill, the only hill for kilometres around then suddenly train tracks. Dam jammed his feet on the tracks and hung on. Just as he felt his arms would be torn off he heard a slight rumbling sound and soon caught the bright yellow light of a locomotive coming through the trees towards him. He saw the pigs stop and blink, their little yellow eyes reflected in the light of the train, their large black shapes stationary as they all stood blinking. Then all at once they squealed and took off again. Dam let go. Their massive black shape rumbled and bumbled along as it sped towards the bushes on the other side of the tracks. The train roared past and Dam turned and walked back to camp. There would be no finding the pigs now they'd be kilometres away and they'd escaped with his net.

There was little he could do until the morning when he could see and follow the tracks. When he arrived back at his camp he noticed there were pig tracks all around his tent.

He crawled inside, zipped up the door and lay down. As he was drifting off to sleep thinking of the next day he sniffed the air. The smell of pigs was very strong. And surely he wasn't breathing quite so heavily. He sat up there was a large black space next to him and a loud breathing sound was coming from it. Dam poked it and it sat up and started grunting! There was a pig in the tent! It began to leap about trying to find a way out. It pulled the tent out of the ground and Dam was rolled over and over.

Eventually Dam found the zip of the door and the pig rushed out into the dark. Dam slept in his car that night he didn't like the thought of being wakened by a large boar coming into the tent.

That night he dreamt he saw a large book with guilt edge pages and a gold embossed cover. It was a very large book and he remembered seeing it on a stand in front of a great herd of pigs or were they people all clapping or were they squealing? He vaguely remembered the title of the book something about flying pigs.

The next day Dam was up early stoking a small fire and making breakfast.

He stretched his tent out and cleaned it for it was full of mud. The herd of pigs had obviously been through his camp on their way to the corn trap.

Luckily Dam had left some corn cobs in his car where they couldn't find them.

Dam set off in the direction of the train tracks and soon he was on the other side trying to work out which way his net had gone. It was impossible, there were so many tracks all running this way and that. After several hours of looking and trying to decipher which ones were which he gave up and turned to go back to his camp.

As he approached the train tracks he heard a faint noise like an approaching wind. And when he looked down the tracks he saw a small dark shape moving along the track. He thought it was a small train coming towards him. He stopped to let it go past. However when it came closer he saw to his amazement that it was large and lumpy and looked remarkably like his landing net full of pigs!

It was his landing net full of pigs and it sailed by honking and grunting with the handle out the back bumping and clanging on the sleepers.

Dam leapt up onto the tracks and began running flat out to catch up to them. The pigs inside the net had worked out how to run quite quickly with the net over them. But not as fast as Dam Diligent, he soon caught up to them and hauled on the handle to slow them down. Seeing Dam the animals let out a unified squeal and took off at full speed. Dam's arms felt stretched three metres longer as he began jumping over two sleepers at a time. He hung on as best he could and hoped that they would soon slow down.

Suddenly one of the pigs let out a very loud noise and the tracks began to vibrate. Dam felt a strange feeling, that something was behind him and he turned to see a huge train bearing down on top of him. Then the loud noise again and he realised it was the train. He let go and dashed off the tracks and the train roared past. After the train had passed Dam couldn't see the pigs anywhere. Maybe they'd been picked up by the train and carried along, he thought! He gave up and began walking back to camp.

On his way he picked up a long stick. He needed one to use as a fishing rod not to catch fish but to catch a pig. Dam had a plan.

That night he put a cob of corn out in the open. Then he made a lasso of rope and encircled the corn with the loop. He then tied the other end of the rope to the end of the stick and climbed his tree again and waited.

He didn't have to wait long before a very large boar with massive tusks came honking along. It was huge and black, Dam had trouble seeing what was mud and what was pig. To get to the corn it walked right underneath Dam in the tree. It gulped the corn down in one mouthful and stood there wagging its tail.

Dam for a split second wondered if the rope would hold the size of it. Nevertheless he grasped the end of the long stick and flung it back with all his might.

He caught the pig! It squealed and took off at full speed. Dam quickly placed the stick in the branches so he didn't have to hold it. The pole bent as though it would break and Dam thought he'd better hang onto the end of it just in case it did. He reached up to try and grab the end of the rope but it was an instant ill-timed for just as he held it the stick broke and he fell to the ground holding the end.

Dam didn't actually hit the ground he landed on something alive. And to his horror he realised he'd hit the landing and it was still full of pigs! He tried to stand but couldn't his feet were caught in the net. There was a little bit of stick left on the end of the other rope with the pig on it and this he wove into the net. Somehow he managed to sit upright as he was bounced and pulled this way and that, the net suddenly taking a violent leap up in the air with dam trying to untwist his feet. With all the squealing and bumping up and down Dam still realised they were travelling in a particular direction – the train tracks.

Dam was stuck, they were carrying him aloft. He'd trapped himself and the huge boar with the tusks was dragging them towards the forest. Dam wrestled with his foot and finally broke free but the other foot was tangled! He could see the train tracks up in front and not far off he could see the yellow light of the train coming nearer.

"Oh, n..n.. no!" he cried as he was bouncing along. Just then a struggle broke out between the large boar and the netted pigs one wanted to go one way and the others wanted to go the other way. Dam just wanted to get off!

And probably because he was on top of the net the large boar eventually won the tug of war. The boar had crossed the tracks and Dam was being dragged towards the train. The bright light looked like a speeding sun about to swallow the earth. Dam was sure he was going to be hit. But luckily when only a few metres away the rope was cut by the wheels and the pack of pigs beneath him quickly spun around grunting and took off down the slope with Dam still leaping about precariously on top.

Gradually they slowed down and began to idle along. They kept Dam suspended above the ground occasionally lowering him depending on the tightness of the net. He began to look out for an overhanging tree limb which he could grab and hopefully pull the entire net off the pack. But they didn't go anywhere near a tree. Dam wrestled with his tangled foot and the pigs seemed to tolerate him as they walked about feeding and doing piggy things.

Dam began to wonder if he'd ever get off. It must have been well past midnight and he was beginning to feel rather like a pig himself. He supposed that with daylight he'd be able to see just how his foot was tangled and be able to release it. So he sat there and lay there and watched the stars. He even grunted a little.

In the net were six large pigs. They all looked like females though Dam couldn't tell. He only wanted to find his car have a drink and go to sleep.

Soon the first light of dawn filtered through the landscape and he began to unwind the threads which held his foot. Soon he was free again and cautiously moved to the side of the net and waited till he was close to a tree and then jumped off. The pigs seeing Dam standing beside them squealed and took off again but not before Dam had tied the cut piece of rope around the tree.

This time he had them, they were trapped.

Because Dam didn't know where he was he began walking in a large spiral in order to find the car. Eventually after about an hour he came across the train tracks and the cut piece of rope. He packed up his camp and drove to the pigs under the net. They were still there lying down asleep. Dam thought he would sleep too so he took out his blanket and lay down beside the car.

Dam and the pigs, his new friends, slept well. The sun was low in the horizon when he awoke. Some of the pigs were standing up looking at him. So Dam began to speak to them in pig language and to us he would have sounded rude. He gave them some corn which they hungrily devoured. Then he found some pieces of rope and prepared himself for the next phase of pig catching.

There was no way he could lift them all up and put them in his car.

He realised he'd have to climb under the net with them and hog tie each one.

He cut six pieces of strong cord and prepared to climb under the net. He threw his blanket over himself so they wouldn't recognise him. He emerged dressed from behind his car and crawled over to them grunting. He lifted the edge of the net and slipped under.

The pigs all stood in a line and sniffed Dam suspiciously. He sat on the other side and waited for them to get used to him again. They watched him intently and he eyed each one and could see thousands of book covers in their eyes. Then to their wonder Dam began to sing. Not your normal song but a piggy song. It went like this

"Snort, snort, grunt, grunt, whistle, grunt, snort, snort." The pigs narrowed their eyes and some batted their eye lids. Then slowly Dam made a lasso and tied the first pig up. It lay on the ground blinking and looking at him. It wasn't long before Dam being diligent had tied up all the others and soon they were all lying on the ground wide eyed looking up at him.

"I won't hurt you" he grunted. Suddenly something disturbed them and they began to make frightened noises. Looking around Dam saw a huge boar with great long tusks peering a him from outside the net. It was the same boar which had escaped from the rope for the rope was still tied to its back leg.

Dam grunted and the pig grunted back. The boar seemed very interested in the other pigs probably, as Dam supposed, because they were female and smelt like corn. Dam looked at the boar and he blinked. Dam didn't like to think that it would be interested in him in the same way. So he grunted and stuck his head out of the blanket. The pig obviously received a terrible fright as it began to snort and toss its head from side to side.

Then Dam realised it was going to charge at him. Quick as he could he lifted up the edge of the net and ran towards the car. He dived in through the window just as a resounding crunch came from the metal below. A large tusk emerged near the driver's seat on the inside of the car. Dam looked out the window and saw that the boar was stuck in the door by its tusks. He jumped out the other side of the car and quickly ran over to the blanket. This he threw over the head of the pig and using the rope already fixed to one of its hind legs hog tied it as quickly as he could. Then he pulled it out of the door.

Dam had seven large pigs. He was very pleased with himself and grunted away merrily as he hauled four up on the roof of his car and tied them down.

He sat two up in the back seat and the large boar he sat next to him. He lashed them all down securely with the safety belts.

Night had fallen by the time he reached the main road. The car was a little heavy but it seemed to take the road and the bumps well. Dam sped home, he was still grunting like a pig. He pulled out a corn cob and began to nibble.

He was dreaming about book covers. As he neared home the blue light of a police car made him pull over and stop.

Dam quickly thought that the boar next to him on the seat was not a good look so he threw his blanket over it.

"Licence please," said the policeman and continued,

"Do you realise you have four pigs tied onto your roof?" Dam grunted then said,

"Oh, sorry officer, yes, I've been talking to a lot of pigs lately!"

Then the policeman saw the pigs sitting up on the back seat.

"Do you realise there are two pigs sitting up on your back seat?"

"Yes," said Dam we have just been to a boaring fancy dress party."

The officer did not reply and simply said,

"Breathe in here."

Dam snorted, grunted, took a breath and blew. The officer then asked,

"Have you been drinking?"

"No," said Dam, "but my wife has, she is feeling a little off colour I think she pigged out on the food!"

With that he took the blanket off the boar and it looked up at the officer and blinked, its tusk just touching the windscreen.

The officer didn't say anything just stood back and gave Dam a horrified look.

They arrived home quite late and Dam drove around the back to his orchard which he had fenced with pig-wire the week before.

There he offloaded the animals and let them go. The great boar jumped to its feet and followed the others.

Dam had grown used to his companions having sung piggy songs to them as he drove home. His grunting fits had become quite profound and I think the pigs were glad to get away from him.

Over the ensuing months Dam fed them well and they settled into their new surroundings and made the orchard grow. Dam produced kilos and kilos of good quality book covers. His piggery soon produced piglets and Dam found himself fully occupied feeding fifty pigs and collecting their manure and making high quality book covers.

The quality of his book covers and binding techniques became legendary and the durability of the covers was outstanding. Dam's 'Pig Manure Books' as he called them were landing orders from big overseas book companies. He was producing history books, encyclopaedias and bibles.

Dam was quite happy grunting away in his workshop. His business had taken off like a wild boar and Dam after all, was anything but boaring.

21

Dam Fights Fire

Dam used to live near a forest and he became quite used to seeing fires on the horizon especially at night. He would watch as the fires grew fiercer in the day time and began to threaten houses.

He often asked himself why the fire authorities didn't put the fire out in the hours after midnight when the fire was at its weakest rather than spend all their energy in the daytime building fire breaks and burning back. Often when the wind was up and the heat of the day was at its worst the fire would break these containment lines and cause panic amongst his friends.

Dam made up his mind to write letters and talk to the fire authorities himself and if that didn't work then he'd go into the bush and put the fire out himself.

He wrote a letter which described a long hose with holes all around its length which could be placed by several men in front of an approaching fire. The water this hose would spray would act like a fire break and help control the blaze.

He described a new sort of footwear which was designed to rake the leaves away like a scrub turkey. These boots had steel blades attached to them to make scratching the ground easier. Dam also invented a new sort of hat which covered a lot of his body. It was made of a fire proof material he found in the bottom of his fish pond. He also made a portable fire-bunker which could be carried in a car or kept at people's homes and erected in moments, if fire threatened. People or families would be able to crawl inside it and be safe from the heat. Dam included in his equipment a knapsack spray which he hoped to fill at selected points along the perforated holy-hose.

He spent considerable amounts of money arranging all this equipment and experimenting in his own kitchen oven with various heat proofing materials.

He saturated an old pair of overalls and gloves with his new heat proof paint and bought a fancy firefighting pump to pump the water through the long hose. Finally he made a large wheel to hold the hose and this he mounted on the roof of his car.

The following summer was hot. The temperature and the winds were rising. Dam listened to the news for word of fire because when there was fire Dam was going off to try out his new gear. He knew his fireproof clothes would work as he'd stood in a few fires in his backyard and he was a wiz with the knapsack spray and his turkey legs were like springs of steel.

Sure enough a fire broke out some distance from his home. It was a hot windy day and the fire was already threatening properties. Dam jumped into his little blue car and was soon screaming like a fire engine. When he arrived he was out of breath from screaming so much and he found the flames were three meters high and were already licking a backyard fence. There were firemen standing ten meters away with their hoses ready.

Dam bounded up dressed in his special hat with his knapsack spray on.

He leapt over the fence in a single bound but misjudged his step at the top of the fence and fell flat on his face on the other side! Unperturbed he bounced up and became a blur of squirting. The fireman had seen what looked like a large white ants nest scurry across the lawn and leap over the fence. They did not know it was a human being. They could not see Dam on the other side of the fence and as the fire diminished they thought they had put out the blaze.

Dam leapt back over the fence and asked to have his knapsack spray filled. The men were horrified. They couldn't see Dam's eyes and thought he was some sort of new species of animal or even a yeti! Whatever they thought his skin had melted. They stood back and were about to put the hose on him when he asked again. The men looked curiously and silently as Dam took his knapsack off and pointed to the water. From behind the veil Dam reassured them that he was actually enjoying himself. The men filled his spray pack and went to watch.

"It was unbelievable!" They recalled. "He was standing in a pile of burning leaves his legs were going like a turkey on train tracks - sparks flying everywhere then the fire was out as quick as that!"

After the blaze was extinguished the fireman looked around for Dam but he had already driven off in a puff of smoke. He was essentially a quiet man who didn't like people asking him silly questions like how did he do it.

In the newspaper the following day the report mentioned how the firemen had put out the blaze in the nick of time. Dam was pleased with that, at least they wouldn't come looking for him. That was okay for the general public but at least a few firemen, who had obviously suffered from extreme heat spoke of a black figure with melted skin who actually put out the fire.

To Dam his fire suit had worked and his firefighting boots too but the real test would come when he tried out his perforated hose and his pump and he didn't have to wait long.

Several fires were out of control in the large area of bushland and if the wind changed it would threaten houses along a wide front. Dam waited till well after dark when the dew was falling. He didn't know that area of bush but he knew he'd have to lie the tube on the downhill side of the approaching fire so the fire would not be inclined to jump the wet area.

At 2:00 am Dam arrived. He connected one end of the hose to his pump near a creek and the other end he grabbed and charged off through the bush. He had three hours to complete the task and he was pretty sure he could stop some of the blaze.

Unfortunately the amount of hose he could fit on his car was not enough to encircle the whole fire. The area he did cover was rapidly extinguished as the flames were only one metre high at the most. If only he had more hose he thought.

When the fire was out it was completely black so he filled his knapsack spray and began to work along the front through the flames. Whenever he could he used natural fire breaks to help him. Things like cliffs and rocks and creeks.

He came back to the hose to refill his spray three times and by the fourth time he was exhausted and the first light of dawn was approaching.

Standing on an outcrop of rock surrounded by smoke he peered out across the green bush which would be all black and smouldering by the afternoon.

Dam hated fires the more fires through an area the hotter the flames each successive time. The bush liked being burnt once every fifteen years or so but not every year that only encouraged trees to die back and allowed fire loving plants to grow.

Dam gave a big sigh and began walking back to his car. He realised there were limitations to his ideas. He hadn't won after all.

As he was rounding a rock he suddenly came face to face with a fireman.

"Eek!" the fireman yelled. "Are you alright!" Dam said he was but the bush wasn't. When he reached his car he found it surrounded by firemen.

Dam walked up to them and began to wind up the holey-hose. The fireman could not believe the length of the hose it was one thousand metres long!

"It's that guy with the burnt skin," said one of the firemen who instantly recognised him.

"Mr Diligent I presume?" said the fire chief.

"Err…yes," said Dam.

"We need your expertise."

"Oh," said Dam.

"Will you let us use your inventions?"

"Of course!" said Dam so long as you stop control burning so often as it makes the fires worse and tell people to plant fire resistant plants around their houses and" he continued, "fight fires after midnight when you've got a real chance to put them out."

"Err yes," said the fire chief and added, "come with me."

Dam sat in the fire truck. They were speeding towards the other end of the fire front. Somebody else was in Dam's little blue car following on behind. Dam was shown a map of the area and where there was water.

"We'll have to go to the water and we need more hose," said Dam.

"It will take you weeks to put all the holes in the hose! Maybe you could have one ready for tomorrow night." He asked the fire chief who was on the phone immediately.

That day Dam and the fire chief watched as the men lit back-burn fires and cleared fire breaks. Dam's work would begin after midnight.

That afternoon the wind came up and the ragged fire front came close to the road which acted as a fire break. At one stage the flames jumped across the road and began to burn ferociously on the other side. The men quickly turned their hoses on it but they couldn't reach it.

Quick as a flash Dam with his knapsack spray jumped over the side and took off through the bush. Several other firemen followed with knapsack sprays but the fire was out by the time they reached Dam.

At 12:00 midnight more holey-hose arrived, about three thousand meters of it!

"We'll use our pumps as well," said the fire chief. The new hose was connected to Dam's old one and together with two other men Dam grabbed the end and stepped into the deep dark night.

Many hours later they emerged and told the men to start the pumps.

Once again he'd put the hose on the downhill side of the approaching fire and this time he'd encircled the whole fire front.

It worked; the main blaze was completely extinguished! Dam took some men along the front with knapsack sprays and extinguished every little spark. Soon a new day was dawning and the fire was out.

Dam was yawning as he drove home in his little blue car.

The fire chief had become his new friend and said he'd be in touch.

Several weeks later "Burnie" as he was called rang up and asked if Dam would sell his inventions to the fire brigade. Dam said he wouldn't because he needed them to fight his own fires and to save his own property. Burnie said they'd use his perforated hose idea and utilize his fire proof paint. And every time they used any of his inventions they would show their respect to Dam by giving him some money. But Dam wasn't interested in money.

As a result of Dam's firefighting efforts the bush fire brigade became revolutionised. Their approach to fighting fires became more successful with fewer lives lost and more property saved.

More importantly to Dam the animals and plants were saved as people learnt to work with nature in the small hours before dawn and not against it in a wild panic when the winds and the heat were at their worst. At those times people's lives and property as well as the good efforts of the firemen were often wasted as the fire leapt over their fire breaks and continued to burn.

22

Dam and the Little Red Racing Car

Dam Diligent had his driving license but it wasn't enough. He wanted to show everybody his knew engine because it was so cheap and clean to run.

In the following few months Dam took a good look at his new red car and decided that the body of it was strong enough to take a crash bar and a larger stronger engine. He looked at the wheels and the steering and went inside to draw up some ideas.

Dam plotted and planned. He drew designs and he balanced weights on rulers. He was redesigning the wheel. If you had looked through the window you would have seen him rolling fruit across the floor, up and down little slopes he had made out of books. Dam was inventing great things.

"I am just a vehicle for my thoughts" he said as he began to demolish his little red car again. He was going to give it independent four wheel steerage.

He was going to change the axils so that the wheels changed angles to the surface of the road and tilted opposite to the direction of the inside of the corner as the car turned. He called this 'vertical axis control.'

Dam made and baked another motor. This one filled the whole back seat of the car. The flywheel in it was mounted horizontally and the motor was suspended from the crash bar by a primitive hook. The motor moved gyroscopically as the vehicle went around corners, so that the weight of the car was thrown to the inside of the turn much like the wheels.

Dam took an old dentist's chair to pieces and made a seat which lay flat in the front of the car. He steered by gripping a lever and looking up at a mirror on the roof which also acted as a wind foil to keep the car on the road.

The whole front of the car Dam converted into the air-intake for the engine while Dam lay in the centre of it. Though the engine was sufficiently cooled and burnt its watery fuel efficiently, Dam knew that 'air in was energy out' as he would say.

From an onlooker's point of view this was quite an unusual car. The wheels were extremely narrow unlike any other racing car and extended a long way out the sides which apart from the mirror on the roof looked like vintage but normal. One unusual difference was that Dam had to crawl underneath it with a match to start it. For it didn't have a battery or a starter switch.

Dam had spent many months preparing his machine. He had devoted himself to it. It was like a seed full of Dam's ideas - a vehicle full of thoughts.

The day drew nearer to the big race where cars from every backyard and engineering shop were entered. There were cars from all over the world all competing for various prizes. There was a prize for the most economical car and another prize for the quietest car; the fastest car and the most environmentally clean car.

Dam had his little red car transported on a trailer to the race track which was one hundred kilometres away near the Olympic stadium and the Fun Park.

Dam was excited he loved going to Fun Parks. He decided to go there if he had time and to the Olympics as well.

The man who had the trailer was amazed at Dam's car and said it looked like a 'garbage truck on bicycle wheels!' Dam didn't mind, he knew that sometimes garbage was capable of great things.

They arrived at the track in the rain and as they slipped about in the mud Dam began to feel anxious that the race would not be held in the wet.

Next day was bright and sunny. The Fun Park was filling up with people. Busses were carrying people to the Olympic stadium and outside the raceway a large traffic jam was slowly beginning to move.

Dam checked his engine. He checked the parachute in the rear and the ropes to open it. Dam was the first to ever use a parachute as a brake and he wondered if it would work.

The time rapidly came for all the cars to approach the line. Dam was nervous. There were some engineering marvels on the line with him. Some resembled space rockets and looked very powerful. Dam felt his hands and they were hot and damp.

Three seconds to go and nobody could work out why there was a fellow in a bright yellow fireproof suit standing behind a garbage truck on the starting line!

The light went green and with a great roar the cars were off. Dam in his luminous yellow fireproof suit took out his flint stones from his pocket and began to strike them furiously.

"Damn!" said Dam for his hands were damp which made it difficult to strike his light. He soon realised he couldn't light his car so he ran over to the crowd calling,

"Matches! Matches!" Luckily somebody threw him a cigarette lighter.

Dam raced back over to his car, dived underneath it and tried the lighter. It did not work!

Poor Dam tried and tried but the lighter would not work! He noticed it had fluid in it so he unscrewed it with his thumbnail and tipped a little fluid on his flint stone.

Dam struck the stones together and there was a massive explosion! He was on fire! As he was putting his gloves back on some men came and put him out even though Dam kept running around trying to avoid them.

Dam looked under his car and luckily his engine was alright. Nothing could stop him now he leapt into the dentist's chair and strapped himself in.

He moved the lever forward and all of a sudden a great wind came rushing up his trouser leg. There was an almighty explosion and a huge ball of yellow flame leapt out of the rear of the car. People hid their faces and held their ears some lay flat on the ground. The men who had put Dam's clothes out threw the hose in the air and ran for cover. And then it happened....

Dam was shot forward so fast that the wind blew his cheeks into a parachute and his eyelashes began flapping like a counting machine.

There was an uncontrollable shaking of the cabin and luckily it bumped his visor down over his face. He tried to see where he was in the mirror but all he could see was an upside down road!

Dam steered as best he could. The people lining the race track became a blur. Dam soon caught up with some cars and passed them so fast that they spun right around. He was coming rapidly to the first corner and realised he had to steer in the opposite way to the way he was seeing because he was looking upside down in the mirror. He was round the bend in an instant as though the steering wheel knew what to do!

"I'm not around the bend after all!" he said. He passed more cars until one car seemed to be the last car and therefore the leader of the race.

Dam was in front but he couldn't work out why his motor had been so noisy. He lay back in his chair and put the accelerator into full throttle. No sooner had he done so than a man with a chequered flag leapt onto the track Dam steered to avoid him and pulled the rope on the parachute. It didn't work! He pulled it again and it still didn't work. Dam was desperate he looked about for a break but he knew he didn't put one in the car.

Then suddenly all the rattling stopped. Everything became very quiet. Dam looked out the side and to his horror realised he was in the sky! He turned the motor off then looked down and saw the Olympic stadium below then suddenly 'bang' he had hit something.

Dam gripped the dentist's chair as he was hurled downwards at a tremendous speed. In his mirror he could make out a whole lot of train tracks and then a carriage full of children went straight underneath him!

As soon as he reached the bottom he was catapulted back up again. Then another carriage passed underneath him. Now Dam was really scarred.

The rattling noise ceased again as Dam was thrust skyward!

"Oh no!" he said as he gripped his dentist's chair in a riveting vertical climb.

"Oh no!" he repeated as he began to plummet back to earth. Dam could see the Olympic pool beneath him and he began to pull desperately on the parachute cord. He felt like a man pulling on the thread of an impossible idea.

To his great relief the parachute opened and he and the car fell through the skylight of a huge building straight into a large swimming pool!

There was another enormous explosion and Dam gripped the dentist's chair and was hurled into another rapid vertical climb. This time to his great relief he was thrown into the Olympic flame, chair and all! Dam unstrapped himself and while still burning stood on the side of the great tower which held the flame.

He held his arms in the air and did a magnificent six point-triple-spin-over jack-fork-knife-spoon tilt into the Olympic pool!

He stayed in the pool for a long time, nobody could work out why. He was treading water in the middle. Dam called out to somebody to throw him a towel then he got out. The fire had burnt his fire proof suit off and he was not properly dressed. Dam emerged with his helmet on and the towel around him.

There was great commotion all about. People were leaning out from the crowd just to touch him. Four policemen came and took him back to the race track.

Dam had won the racing car race but had caused a lot of damage. Bits of Dam's car were imbedded in the roof of the Olympic stadium and the loop in the roller coaster had been straightened flat. Luckily the prize money was enough to repair the damage. And nobody was injured.

People came from all over the world to ask Dam about his car. He would entertain them all and begin to balance weights on rulers and roll fruit around the floor. They all thought he was around the bend especially since Dam still hadn't taken his crash helmet off! They looked at him in a strange way when he said,

"It was a vehicle full of thoughts. Difficult to steer but I got around the bend!"

23

Dam and the Butcher

Dam was very fond of dogs. He spoke to them quite often in their own language. Sometimes to amuse his favourite butcher he would bark and whine whenever he entered the shop. This usually allowed him to be served first.

One day Dam was looking through the newspaper when he noticed an advertisement for a new butcher shop in town. The add read,

'Mrs Dripping's Hop and Gary's Butcher Shop – New - Specialising in Sausages.' Dam was feeling hungry already and the next shopping day he decided to pay the new shop a visit.

Now it so happened that one of Dam's friends had gone on holiday and Dam was minding this person's dog for a few days. Dam also decided to buy the dog some bones.

He and the dog jumped in the car and were on their way one Saturday morning to have a look at the new butchers shop.

Hop and Gary's Butchers Shop was in the main street and fortunately for Dam there was a parking spot right outside the shop. Dam turned to the dog and gave a little whine which meant,

"I'll be back soon with a huge bone!" Dam wound the window down and the dog stuck its head out and then its tongue.

Dam jumped out of the car and looked in the window of the shop. There was a sign which read 'Sausages on Special.' A little bell above the door tinkled as he entered. Nobody was serving.

There were sausages everywhere, some were huge and some were long and skinny. The sausages on special looked green and a little old to Dam.

He reached over onto the counter and rang the bell. He rang the bell again but nobody came. Then he barked loudly.

All of a sudden a red faced man ran out of the back room so fast he banged his hand on a knife which was stuck in a large block of wood near the doorway.

The man swore and grabbed the wound with his other hand. Not looking at Dam he leaned right over the counter and surveyed the floor.

"Where's that dog!?" He growled.

"No dog," said Dam. "Mr Hop I presume?"

"Yes," said Mr Hop attending to his wound. "What can I do for you?"

"I'd like some fresh sausages and some bones for my dog please."

"No dogs in here!" said Mr Hop.

"Dog's in the car," said Dam and added, "Nice day."

Mr Hop then began to handle the green sausages and ask Dam how many he would like. Dam said he didn't want those ones and asked about some other sausages which were displayed in the window. Mr Hop was having trouble with his wound.

"These are fresher," said Mr Hop, "they've been seasoned with parsley that's why they're green."

"Oh," said Dam "but I think I'd like those over there" he said pointing to others in the window.

The butcher began to gather several from the pile in the window when Dam spied some fresher looking ones next to them.

"Oh they look better," he said.

Mr Hop began to gather some of those saying,

"One pound or what?" to which Dam replied,

"Oh about a kilo."

The butcher gathered several up and was in the process of wrapping them when Dam changed his mind again.

"Oh!" he said, "I am sorry, I might try the green ones, if you say they are fresh."

"Well have a look." said Mr Hop and cut one in half and threw it to Dam.

Dam caught it and held it to his nose. It smelt bad. Dam threw it back to Mr Hop but unfortunately it hit him in the eye! Mr Hop received such a shock he became angry and hurled the sausage back at Dam!

Dam being Diligent ducked and the sausage hit the wall. The butcher then threw another and Dam caught it and threw it back. It hit him in the other eye!

Suddenly a great string of green sausages came hurtling through the air at Dam! The butcher had gone hopping mad!

Dam left the shop. Sausages were hitting the wall and flying all around him. He opened the door and the little bell tinkled. Fortunately a customer was just entering the shop so Dam held the door open. Just then a long skinny sausage flew past his nose and hit the lady who was entering. It landed fair in her face and stayed there draped over her nose! Dam noticed flecks of blood on it from the butcher's wound.

"Oh! Mrs Dripping!" he heard the butcher say.

Mrs Dripping entered the shop and slipped on a sausage and fell fair and square on her behind!

By this time the dog in the car was barking loudly. Dam left but not before he barked a few times too.

"I'm not going back to that shop!" he said to the dog in doggy language.

"It was a bit wuff in there!" He looked up at the sign and said,

"Hopping, Dripping, Gangrene's Angry Butchers Shop!" he said.

Dam went to his old butchers and bought some nice fresh sausages and a large bone for the dog.

24

Dam and the Christmas Tree

Dam's voice was growing hoarse, he'd been yelling for an hour.

The Christmas tree was giving him hay-fever, Dam had suspected for ages that he was allergic to pine trees. Most of the people singing in the church grounds were entirely out of tune so Dam found he had to sing very loudly to keep the choir in key.

Dam found himself yelling 'thought I'd fooled ya' when others were singing 'Allehlooolya!' and it was when they paused on the 'ooo' as in 'Allehloooo' that Dam felt a sneeze coming on but forgot to take a breath. He began to feel giddy and was sure he saw the mighty Lord himself or was it angels, bedecked in stars, come springing out of the giant Christmas tree. One of them wacked Dam on the head with her star stick and he crashed to the ground!

Dam dreamt he was hunting wild boar with his spear again and began to make wild boar noises on the ground. There was a particularly large beast quite close, he could smell it though it was so dark he couldn't tell where it was. Suddenly the blackness disappeared and he realised the boar was only a few feet from him and he'd been looking straight at it! He charged off after it, making loud grunting noises. For some reason a star had stuck itself on the end of his spear and he couldn't get rid of it!

Soon the darkness cleared and he was surrounded by a lot of really old angels. Some of whom seemed incredibly ugly. Then he realised he was on the ground and the rest of the choir were leaning over him!

"He's had a stroke!" one said.

"Thank God!" said another.

Dam stretched his legs out, lay on his back, crossed his hands on his chest and smiled. He hadn't been boar hunting since he was a young boy. He wished he was deep in his cave with his spears by his side and the smell of wild boar under his fingertips.

Just then a man with a cap on his head came and bent over him.

"How are you feeling?" he asked. Dam replied,

"Boared"

"Bored!" said one of the women.

"He's anything but boring! He drove me here at one hundred miles an hour on the wrong side of the road! Half way here he said,

"Could you hold this? And produced a snake out of his pocket! This fellow is crazy singing like that! Give anybody a heart attack!"

"I'm alright," said Dam rising to his feet. "I don't need to go to horse-piddle, which was Dam's word for hospital."

With that he floated over to a seat under the Christmas tree and sat down to watch the choir singing their Christmas carols. He still wished he was hunting wild boar. Dam soon recovered and began to feel a little bit mischievous.

As quick as a flash he sprang up into the tree and began to move steadily along its branches. The choir couldn't see him as the multitude of little lights in the tree blinded their view. Dam didn't like the smell of pine trees and began collecting lots of small pine cones and lobbing them down into the choir.

Unfortunately one or two found some open mouths and a few women started coughing, spluttering and gasping for air! Then Dam started sneezing, he was reacting to the sap in the pine cones and the tree began to shake. The woman who Dam had given a lift to spied him in the tree and screamed,

"There he is, in the tree!" The other choir members thought she'd seen God or Santa Claus.

"Yes Mary," they said quietly "No!" she exclaimed, "it's that Diligent fellow, Dam Dilli-Diligent!"

Dam slipped out the back of the tree and jumped onto the roof of the building. He bounded over it like a monkey and grabbed hold of a chimney on the outside and slid down into the first window. It was somebody's bathroom and there on the shelf Dam spied a spray can of deodorant.

"Just what I need," he said as he shinnied back up the chimney and onto the roof. He peeped over its rim at the group of singers in the yard who by this time seemed to have settled down.

Dam crept back into the Christmas tree. The temptation to sneeze was very great. He put the can of deodorant in a fork of the tree and left the nozzle on so it sprayed continuously. Then he climbed down the tree holding his nose and dropped back onto his seat.

At that stage the choir of angels began singing one of Dam's favourite songs and feeling somewhat uplifted he stood up and began walking back over to join them. But alas his legs became hopelessly entangled in the electric lights cord. He shook one leg and then the other. Suddenly the lights in the tree began to flicker on and off and sparks began to fly this way and that about his legs until Dam was dancing in a halo of sparks!

"I can see him now!" cried Mary.

"Help!" cried Dam, "it's biting me!" Just then a three foot long snake leapt out of Dam's pocket and slithered into the choir. Pandemonium broke out and Dam called out,

"Eevy! Don't leave me now!" Suddenly there was a loud fizzing sound from the Christmas tree behind the choir. He looked up just in time to see the sparks rise up and the whole Christmas tree explode in a great ball of flame!

There were loud bangs and whizzes of sparks like fire crackers sprayed up from the tree! The choir received such a shock they all ran in towards each other screaming in a single note and all knocked each other to the ground!

Mary was sure she saw Dam's hair stand on end as he raced over to them trailing electrical cord and calling,

"Eevy! Eevy!" People on the ground were exclaiming

"Good Lord!"

"Oh my God!" and

"Jesus Christ!"

"Allehlooolya!" Dam yelled as he did the sparkling stomp amongst them. Occasionally lifting up their bodies to see if his snake was underneath.

One woman yelled out,

"You're on fire!" Dam looked into her eyes and said,

"You're pretty good yourself!" Suddenly one woman shrieked and began holding her dress down. Dam thinking Eevy was underneath tried lifting it up!

Poor Dam received a powerful blow to his left eye which temporally blinded him and knocked him out like a light. He lay on the ground again grunting with a smile!

Then somebody threw a bucket of water over him!

Well you should have heard the singing then! Obviously whoever threw the water over the choir didn't realise that water conducts electricity! The people still on the ground shot to their feet like lightning and they all began doing a highland jig! Somebody was heard to say,

"Oh forgive me!"

Eventually everything settled down. Dam was singing to himself even though half his clothes were burnt off and he was finding it difficult to see out of one eye and he couldn't find his snake anywhere. While blinking and squinting his sore eye he asked Mary if she wanted a lift home.

She was still suffering from shock as she sat in the car beside him, thoroughly saturated saying, "Lord! Lord!" over and over again. Dam was finding driving with one eye quite difficult.

Half way home Mary let out a piercing scream and Dam nearly lost control of the wheel! What do you think Mary had found in her pocket?

"Eevy!" cried Dam delightedly. "You've come home!"

25

Dam Writes a Letter

Dam had not written to Lilly for several hours. He was in the habit of writing a little something every hour because he was so in love. He sat down at his window seat and stared out at the tadpoles rising and falling in his dam several meters below. As he was musing he drifted off and dreamt he was a tadpole rising up to take a breath. The moment he reached the surface he banged his head on the table and woke up. As his head went down his eye found the pen he was holding in his hand, poised to write. He woke with a start and after checking his eye to see if he could still see, he began to write.

"My darling Lilly, I've just jabbed myself in the eye with my pen thinking I was a tadpole rising up to kiss your surface."

"She'll like that," he said to himself. He was becoming quite a letter writer and was discovering poetry. He often reflected on the camping trip they had together, looking for gold and how his gold tooth had fallen down her throat the very first time he went to kiss her and the difficulty they both had trying to find it.

He kept writing, "When looking at beauty in a mirror remember to look behind." And further on, "Tadpoles make me feel like croaking!"

Lilly was quite a different sort of letter writer to Dam and in each letter she always mentioned burning toast and the fact that she hated cooking but was very fond of eating. Dam hadn't seen her for years and he wondered how she looked.

"Please send me a photograph of yourself," he would often write. However a picture never came only the memories of her smile.

Dam wrote quite a lot that day. He mentioned how one eye was lonely for the other and how it was dripping tears onto the page while being held shut with his free hand. The eye which could see, never the less, was 'Blinded by the happiness of love,' he wrote.

Finally he folded the letter and addressed it and rode his new bicycle the four kilometres to post it in the new letterbox at the end of the road. The day was sweet. Love seemed to make everything new and beautiful.

Apart from his writing which explored his ideas, Dam was fond of inventing all sorts of things. One of his latest inventions was his bicycle.

He was very proud of it as it was the culmination of much thought and engineering skill. He called it his 'jump bike' and jump it did.

It consisted of a seat mounted on a bow-like spring which had a wheel at each end. The axle of each wheel was as eccentric as Dam, so that each time he bounced down on the seat the wheels would turn. To make the contraption move was quite easy, all one had to do was bounce up and down. And if one bounced rapidly the bike would tear along at a phenomenal rate. The only problem was that the rider was forced to go up and down with the bike.

To steer it one had to lean to the side one wanted to go. This required a little practice before one got it right.

When going down a hill at high speed, one had to keep one's jaw closed because more than once Dam had nearly bitten his tongue off. Dam had to make a special seat as he'd injured himself terribly the first time he'd ridden it and after a while decided that it was really a ladies bike.

Dam's eye was still quite sore as he took off down the road. He became quite excited about posting the letter and began to jump a little. With the letter clenched between his teeth he began prancing down the road.

Suddenly a wallaby darted out from the bushes. It nearly slammed straight into Dam. However it turned sideways and miraculously bounded along beside him. It was so close to him it turned its head and they looked each other in the eye as each one bounced simultaneously.

Dam said,

"Hell...o, how... are... you?" between his teeth and the wallaby lunged sideways narrowly missing the bike's back wheel. Around the next corner Dam came upon a fallen tree across the road. With a single bound he leapt two meters in the air. Dam had been known to jump five meters in the air so this obstacle was no obstacle at all.

Dam arrived safely at the post-box it was one of those fancy new red ones. They'd installed it a few weeks earlier and cemented it into the road.

Dam popped the letter in and was just about to get back on his bicycle when he remembered he'd forgotten to put a stamp on it. And then again he was unsure if he'd addressed it correctly. He recalled writing Kissing Point Road, that always gave him tingles down the spine but couldn't remember if he'd written the post code.

He went back and peeped through the hungry black hole where he'd put the letter. Fortunately the tip of it was still visible so he reached in and tried to grasp it, however he dislodged it and it slipped further in!

"Damn!" said Dam as he tried to pull his fingers out of the hole.

"Damn!" he said again as he realised his hand was stuck. He pulled and tugged and wiggled his fingers but alas his hand was jammed. He stopped for a moment to think about it but soon began pulling and yanking frantically.

He spoke to the box nicely; pleading with it to let go. It did not answer.

He became angry with the hole and hurt his hand. After a while he looked at his poor fingers through the small nasty slit. They looked as though they were swollen!

Pretty soon the night closed down around him. A car went by and Dam waved in distress with his left hand. The car waved back and kept driving.

He slept that night on his knees in front of the letter box with his hand up in the cold hole. He didn't sleep much and sometimes rested leaning his head on its cold metal breast.

All night he kept trying to pull his hand out but it seemed well and truly stuck. He wished he was home in his little bed tucked up listening to the sound of his frogs in the dam. He ceased waving at cars, none stopped. He knew the postman would come around ten o'clock in the morning. He began to feel hungry. When the postman finally arrived the hot sun was blazing down and Dam was thirsty.

"Oh," said Dam, "I'm stuck!"

"Stuck!?" said the postman as he opened the box from the other side and looked in. "Yes you are stuck!" he said. "What are you going to do?" Dam said he didn't have a clue what to do but he was sure he wasn't going to die a victim of a letter box.

The postie laughed, got back in his car and drove off saying,

"I'll see what I can do." Dam spent all that day and another night stuck in the letter box! When the postman arrived the next day he found Dam in a lighter mood.

"Gooday mate!" said Dam. "I've spent two days and two nights intimately connected to your lovely letter box! It's been a real holiday. I've had no lawns to mow, no meals to cook and no dishes to wash. I've had some wonderful conversations with acquaintances who have most kindly given me their mail to post; and how are you this fine summer's day? Obviously not stuck in a box?"

The mailman scratched his chin and opened the box and looked at Dam's fingers again. He reached up and grabbed one and tried pushing it out the other way.

"Argh!" cried Dam, "Don't do that!"

"What can I do?" said the postman. "Your fingers are terribly swollen.

You might start bleeding all over my mail!" Dam stern faced looked at him and said,

"I am Dam Diligent, I don't bleed. I can hold my blood in."

"I'll talk to my boss." said the postman as he revved his engine and was gone again.

Dam was alone and leant on the post-box, even hugged it and said,

"I love posting letters!"

Not long afterwards a car pulled up and a lady emerged with a large parcel. Because Dam's hand was in the way the parcel would not fit in the box.

"Oh you poor man!" she said and promised to ring the relevant authorities.

Dam fought with his fingers once again and banged on the box with the other hand and called out saying,

"Let go!" But it didn't.

That afternoon a car arrived with an official sort of man inside.

"You alright mate?" he asked Dam.

"Fine!" said Dam, "I'm starving! I've been here for three days, standing up.

I haven't had any sleep and I'm dying!"

"Okay, I'll see what I can do." He got back in his car and drove off.

Dam was alone again and spent another night in the cold standing up. He didn't get much sleep.

The next day at 10:00 the postman arrived. Dam didn't say a word.

The postie said,

"Good morning." He looked up at Dam's fingers and said,

"They're looking green today" and drove off. Soon after that, the same woman arrived with the same parcel.

"Oh no!" she said and promised again to ring the authorities as she drove off.

The same cars drove by and Dam resumed waving. They all waved back and kept going.

"Lovely day!" Dam said under his breath. Late that afternoon a Council truck arrived and three men climbed out. They asked Dam if he was the person who had tried to climb in the letter box.

They then proceeded to unload the truck. They had a compressor and a jack hammer and were soon smashing up the concrete around the letter box.

After some time the red monster was free though it was still munching on Dam's hand and with some difficulty they threw him and the letter box in the back of the truck. As Dam bounced along in the back, he wondered if he'd ever go near a letter box again. He sat next to it with one arm around it like an old friend for it was difficult not to jar his fingers when they went over bumps.

The truck travelled the twenty kilometres into the Council Works depot where everybody came to look at the man who tried to climb into a letter box. Finally the nasty metal opening was widened with oxy cutting equipment and Dam's hand was free. He flexed his fingers.

"Oh thank you!" he said to the letter box.

The men said goodbye and left him there; he was alone again. It was growing dark and Dam walked out onto the road to try to get a lift. Nobody stopped.

One car even waved at him and kept driving. He recognised the car, it was the woman with the parcel.

Dam walked all through the night and at about 10:00 in the morning he was just coming over the hill to his road when some distance off he noticed the postman arriving to collect the mail. The postman got out of his car, walked over to the hole where the post box had been and looked around. Spying Dam's bicycle he picked it up, looked around again and was gone, bicycle and all.

Dam walked all the way home. He fed himself and went to bed where he slept for the rest of that day and into the night. Next day he wrote a letter to Lilly. This time he put a stamp on it. He walked down to the corner and waited for the postman to arrive. There was already a nice new letter box cemented in the road with its hungry black mouth open waiting for letters,

"Like a shark," thought Dam.

At 10:00 the postman arrived and he climbed out very slowly. He had a bandage around his head, a black eye and his arm was in a sling.

He was considerably bent over as he hobbled over to the post box.

"Orring" he said to Dam who noticed immediately that he'd bitten his tongue. Dam asked the postie for his bicycle back.

"Iceycle? Ooo, eess, oo orrow." And added, "Ee oo." He climbed into his car very slowly after checking the post box with his good hand.

The next day Dam was at the post box at 10:00 and it wasn't long before the postie arrived with Dam's jump bike in the car. He was still all bandaged up.

"Oood orring" the postie said. But Dam said nothing. The postie handed Dam some mail and said,

"I eek eek afe or ooo." Dam helped the postie take his bike out of the car. Dam was still silent.

The postman drove off. Dam looked at his letters. One was from Lilly so he bounded home very fast to open it. The first thing which popped out was a photograph of a strange person. Lilly said she had been severely electrocuted while trying to prize some burnt toast out of the toaster when her fingers had become stuck in it and her face had melted! And why hadn't Dam written a letter to her for five days?

The other mail was from the postal authorities asking Dam to pay for the new letter box and its installation, also a letter from Council asking him to pay for the three men who broke up the concrete, gave him a lift into town and to pay for the oxy cutting which freed Dam's hand.

Dam sat down at his desk and looked at the photograph. He looked out to his dam and watched the tadpoles rising like his tears to the surface to take a breath where they made ripples like fingers on delicate skin.

26

Dam Plays the Cello

Late one afternoon Dam decided to listen to the radio. He turned the power on and put the volume up high for he wanted to hear it out in his garden as he watered his beans. The sky overhead was ragged with clouds and he could smell the rain. Ants were active on the ground but Dam being diligent kept watering away. The beans were growing quite long and he wanted to fatten them up.

As he was watering he heard some strange lilting music coming from the sky - no, from the bushes, no - as he listened more intently, it was the radio. Somebody was playing the cello. He had never heard it played before and he turned the hose off and listened as he watched the sky prepare for rain.

Dam drifted off. He was swaying like his beans, when the low notes came he would rock forwards and when the high notes came he would rock from side to side. He stayed that way, quite transfixed until the first rain drop hit him in the eye.

The music stopped and his beans stood still. Dam rolled up the hose and went inside. As the rain beat down on the tin roof he went to the phone book and looked up musical instrument shops. He was going to learn how to play the cello.

The only music shop he could find was some distance down the coast. So he decided to take a short holiday to his favourite fishing spot on the way. The next day he packed his rods in the car and motored into town where he brought some supplies and some brand new fish hooks. He was excited, not only was he going to catch a great big fish but he was going to buy a friend, which would sing to him!

In the afternoon of the next day he arrived at the music shop and went inside. There were cellos in there, great big ones. They were so large he wondered how he'd fit it in the car. He sat down in the shop and was shown how to hold the instrument and the bow.

Dam took a stroke and his back shivered. He took another stroke and his back shivered again! There were ten cellos in the shop and Dam stroked each one. The last one he tried was the best, its note was pure and long and Dam's back was shivered silly. He bought that one. He grabbed it in his arms like a long lost friend and tied it to the roof of his car. He drove down to the beach.

The place he wanted to fish from was some distance around the headland right on the tip of the outermost rock. There was a gentle swell on the surf beach where Dam had pitched his tent. After a small meal he took his cello out of the great big case and went down near the sand. He found a nice round rock to sit on and there by the light of the quarter moon he played his first symphony.

The moon arched across the sky and Dam's bottom was stony cold. All time stood still for him as he was transported off into other realms. The sound of the sea accompanied him. At one stage the waves seemed to move in time to his playing and various crabs all gathered like an audience and watched his every move.

"If this thing attracts crabs" he said, "it may attract fish." When the tide came in and was washing about his feet he picked up his instrument and went up to his tent. With the sound of the cello still on his mind he drifted into a stony sleep, intent on waking up early the next morning to go fishing.

Dam woke at midday.

"Damn!" said Dam as he wiped his eyes; he'd missed the best time to fish. Even before his breakfast he took the cello out of its case and began to play. The sun was high and the day quite warm. Immediately a flock of small birds came and sat on his tent and watched him. They were most inquisitive and jumped onto the grass in front of him. They seemed intrigued by the sound and kept dancing about. The sun was too hot and Dam prepared to go fishing that afternoon.

During the day he convinced himself that his cello would attract fish as well. After all it had attracted crabs and birds so why not fish? Late that afternoon he picked up his fishing rod and fishing basket. Then he threw the cello onto his shoulder for the long walk. He was off. After some difficulty he finally arrived on the last rock, his favourite fishing spot. The sea was very smooth and the tide was coming in. There was a slight swell, which made the rocks pop and hiss with all the life clinging to them.

Way out there on the end of the headland was almost like being out at sea.

He could see the beach stretching to the north and the other misty headlands in the far away distance. Looking around he found a perfect place to sit and play the cello.

Dam bowed a few notes and cast his eyes on the sea. He stroked some more and then became completely entranced and played and played. Occasionally he looked at the sea and thought he saw the huge eyes of fish watching him.

He didn't mind, why should he catch and kill them when they too liked the cello?

Dam didn't see the school of tuna stop on their way around the headland and come in very close and stay dead still as they listened. Nor did he see the black drummer come to the surface and peep out and wave their fins at him.

Dam didn't even notice the huge blue groper which came right up to the rock he was on and turn on its side and wave its fins out of the water. Dam kept playing he was sort of in a trance. The sun dipped below the horizon and the sea turned to molten gold.

Just then a large rock appeared on the shoreline. Dam watched it curiously. It was half as big as the cello and was moving slowly towards him. In the orange glow he realised it was an octopus. He could see its large black eyes staring at him. Its tentacles were spread all about and their tips were swaying with the sounds. Dam kept his eyes on it as it moved closer and closer. When he played a high note the octopus waved its tentacles to the left and when he played a low note all the frilly tentacles danced to the right. The octopus was dancing to the sound of the cello. It did not come any closer.

As he played more and more the octopus began to rise up on its tentacles and sway from side to side. Dam was overcome with joy and suddenly stopped playing and said,

"You're dancing!" Dam could hear the splash and lap of the waves. He could hear the spit, pop and hiss of the sea creatures around him. Then he realised it was dark and the moon was high in the sky. Slowly the octopus crept back into the water and disappeared. Dam picked up his rod and cello and began the long walk home. He was hungry but he didn't mind, he hadn't caught any fish but he'd made an octopus dance.

27

Dam and the Apple Tree

Dam liked apples they were his favourite fruit. In shops he flicked them to see how crisp they were. His fingers were as strong as the kick of a horse and the fruit shop man soon learnt that Dam had to buy every apple he flicked for each one developed a large bruise on it afterwards.

Dam sprouted an apple tree seed and watched it grow into a tree. He fed it ant droppings and these he collected by allowing ants to feed on a large sheet of paper. He thought that a certain type of bacteria which fed on the ant droppings also fed the apple tree and quite soon his apple tree thanked Dam by growing healthily and huge. "It's not big enough," Dam said. So he set about making a compost heap to feed it. He put all his vegetable scraps in the heap and collected lots of grass clippings, leaves, branches, old shoes, clothes, cardboard, newspapers, pieces of wood and road-kills. The latter he collected on his fortnightly trips into town. He found lizards and frogs, birds and rabbits, foxes and snakes. Anything that was dead on the road he buried in his compost heap. Over time the heap grew and grew. Dam bought bags of pig and chook manure and fed that to the tree as well. The apple tree grew as tall as a house and eventually set blossom. It was a beautiful tree covered in flowers, large pink ones. Dam spent many an hour sniffing them and watching the bees feasting on the nectar.

Soon the summer growth began and the small green shoots developed into leaves and some of the blossom developed into apples. Dam's excitement grew as the apples grew. One night however there was a strong wind and many of the small apples were knocked off the tree. Dam was disappointed as he watched his tree flourishing with only one apple left!

"One is better than none!" he said as he lay beneath the tree and watched the apple grow. There was something odd about this apple though and as he watched each day Dam soon realised that it was a double apple, not one but two joined together.

"This is most unusual," he said as he fed the tree more compost. The apples grew larger and larger until they were the size of tennis balls. They were still green however and Dam wondered when they would be ready to pick. For some reason, Dam couldn't work out why, the apple or apples grew astonishingly large. Both apples became the size of Dam's head and looked kind of like Dam's head though they were green and bald. They became so heavy the branch they were on was weighed down.

He rang the Agricultural Department and they laughed at him when he described the size of the apples and the fact that they were joined together.

All they said was,

"Bring them in and show us when you pick them."

One day Dam lay down under his apple tree and looked up at the huge apples. They were the size of basketballs and looked positively delicious with a slight yellowish tinge and now a touch of orange. As he watched them swaying in the gentle breeze his eyes became sleepy. Just as he was about to doze off there was a loud swooshing noise and the apples fell off and landed square on Dam's stomach! Dam was winded, he was in pain. He received such a shock he sat bolt upright but soon lay down again. Dam's ribs were broken he was lucky to be alive!

He lay there for some time unable to move with the huge apples beside him.

He moved his legs and rolled over. What was he going to do? Lunch time passed and then dinner came along. Two ants climbed on top of one apple and to Dam it looked like they were fighting for the prize of the apple. Dam reached out and separated them and put one on each apple. He felt hungry and looked at his apples, they looked very appetising. He moved closer and sank his teeth into one of them. The sweet juice of a beautiful fresh apple poured down his throat and he felt refreshed.

With a great effort Dam climbed to his knees and began to crawl to his house. He managed to reach the door handle and crawl into his bedroom where he crawled up onto his bed and crawled into sleep. Dam knew he had to be still to mend his ribs. When he woke up in the morning he felt a lot better and wondered about his apples and how they had spent the night. He moved around a little but it was no good he felt he needed to go to horse-piddle (hospital). Dam said damn as he fumbled for the keys to his car. Damn he said again as he realised he'd have to collect and protect his apples for scientific reasons.

He picked up a broom to use as a crutch and wobbled into his car.

Fortunately he could drive down to his orchard and was very relieved to find the apples still there under the tree. Even the ants were still battling on one of the apples. Dam separated them again and put them on the ground. He crawled around the back of the car and lifted up the boot. Then he put the broomstick in between the apples and with a great effort lifted them up. The apples rolled down the stick and fell into the boot. Dam then crawled into the car and drove into town very slowly.

On the way, even though he was driving slowly, he managed to run over a cat! Being in the habit of collecting road kills he stopped the car and crawled out to see if it was alright. Unfortunately it was dead so Dam threw it in the boot with the apples.

"Horse-piddle again," said Dam "I hate the horse-piddle." When he arrived he crawled up the stairs and wobbled along the corridor.

"What is it this time, Mr Diligent?" said the very Slow-nurse. Dam had placed some match sticks across his tongue so he said,

"I…oken… aye…ibbs" and stuck out his tongue. The very Slow-nurse on seeing the match sticks shrieked with laughter. People came flying out of doors asking what was wrong. Dam took his matches out and puffed up his cheeks and looked green. He staggered over to a chair.

"Oh my apples!" he said to himself as he sat down and added, "I'm dying!"

The very Slow-nurse stopped shrieking and peered inquisitively down at Dam who looked up and noticed she was even larger at the front than when he was on the same level as her.

Presently a Docked-door (doctor) came and stood beside them.

"How did you do that to yourself?" the Slow-nurse was asking.

"My apples fell out of the tree and squashed me."

Well the Slow-nurse wobbled frighteningly with laughter. She was used to Dam's humour.

"You absolutely crack me up!" she said. To which Dam replied under his breath,

"Cracked already!"

The Docked-door glanced at the Slow-nurse and said,

"At least you're cracked in the right place."

Dam moaned,

"My apples, they're huge and joined together. I was nearly asleep and they fell on my stomach and broke some ribs." He looked around for somewhere to throw the matches.

"You will need an x-ray?" said the Docked-door.

"New ribs would be better!" Dam replied.

Dam was helped into a room and laid on a table. The Docked-door poked and prodded him almost everywhere and Dam started giggling. He hated being tickled and he called out,

"Stop!" but the Docked-door kept pushing him here and there and tickling. Dam's jaw began to gnash. It was a spontaneous reaction which his body did whenever he was tickled. He found this out early in life when a girl at school tickled him under the arm. Dam was eating his lunch at the time and it went everywhere.

In the end Dam said to the Docked-door,

"Ah..ha..ha, I…like…your…ring, m…may I see?" Dam held the Docked-door's hand close to his face then all at once lunged forward and bit it savagely. Dam hated being tickled!

That stopped the Docked-door well and truly. He didn't know what to say! Dam's teeth stopped gnashing and he looked innocent and naughty. He was good at that. The Doctor-door remembering his call said he didn't think Dam's ribs were broken and he didn't need an x-ray after all.

The Docked-door left the room rather quickly holding his hand. Dam sensed he was not happy and had probably gone somewhere to sterilize it.

"Just a little bit - a little bit of a bite," said Dam to himself.

He crawled out of the room past the awfully Slow-nurse. She was under the counter doing something. All Dam could see was her curly hair and funny half-hat. He threw the matches on her head. She didn't even notice. He staggered back to his car. He was feeling a little bit better. He lifted up the boot to check the apples and there upon one of them was the same pair of ants, again doing battle! On the other apple was the dead cat. Dam put the ants on the side of the boot and decided to go back inside the horse-piddle and show the Docked-door and the very Slow-nurse his apples. For he felt a little sorry for the Docked-door having mauled his hand.

Dam put a towel around the apples and lifted them up but not before he had sunk his teeth into them again.

"Just a little bit of a bite," he said and added, "Oh they are nice!" as he took yet another bite.

Dam put his huge green apples on the front desk. The Slow-nurse's eyes lit up. The matches were still in her hair where they balanced precariously as she slowly talked.

"Ooh! What enormous apples! Did you grow them yourself?" She said very slowly. Dam thought she was joking so he told the truth,

"No, they grew on a tree which I fed with road-kills!" Then thinking the horse-piddle may be a good place to obtain compost from, he asked, "Do you have any road-kills?" and added. "Would you like a bite?"

"No, thank you," she said, "You've already been eating them!"

"But it's large enough for you to have a fresh bite too," Dam rhymed.

"Oh alright, I'll bite a bit." She said as she sank her teeth into one.

"Oh!" she said. "How delicious! Does the other one taste the same?"

Quick as a flash, before Dam could move them aside, her extendible jaws savaged another chunk. Dam looked at the piece she'd taken out and the extraordinarily gross size of her gobbling mouth. She spoke with her mouth full and dribbles of saliva ran down her chin and dribbled on the desk!

"Err," said Dam. Then spying the Docked-door flit from one door to another, called out.

"Oh Docked-door come and see this, would you like a bite? And I'm sorry I bit you, you were tickling me!"

"What's this then, poisonous?" the docked-door asked.

"Delicious huge apples!" said the Slow-nurse who seemed to be speeding up.

"As big as your b.." The Docked-door stopped short of saying anything as he peered across at her. "I love apples," he continued, "Oh, I'll have a little bit of a bite, thank you."

"Be my guest," said Dam. With that the Docked-door lent across the desk and took a large bite.

"Oh," he said, "that's delicious. Does the other one taste the same?" It was too late, he was taking a bite of the second one before Dam could whisk them away. Dam was horrified by the size of the chunks they had both taken out.

The Docked-door also ate with his mouth open and drooled on the floor.

His bite was enormous! Dam was disgusted!

It wasn't long before another nurse who was wandering by, spied the large green lumps on the desk and came over to have a look. And it wasn't long before she lunged forward and sank her teeth into a fresh patch as well!

Funny how people do that with apples Dam thought.

He looked about him. There were three people staring at his apples now, all ready to sink their fangs and take a bite. Dam wrapped them up quickly in the towel and made a hasty retreat. Nobody thanked him and nobody helped him as he staggered outside.

On his way out a young boy stopped him and asked if he could have a bite.

Dam quite liked young children so he said he could.

Well you should have seen the size of the chunk this small boy took out of the apples!

The boy's mouth could barely move as he said,

"Ank oo." Dam felt wounded. He quickly left. One leg felt a bit shorter as though his foot had been bitten off.

"Typical horse-piddle," he said. "Go in sick and come out feeling as though you've been mauled by sharks."

When Dam got back to the car he revealed the apples and studied the extent of the damage. "Greedy people!" he said as he took another bite. And just to be different he took a massive bite a second time and nibbled bits on the way to the Agricultural Department.

Dam had not gone far when he spied another dead cat on the side of the road. He stopped the car and threw it in the boot with the apples. Further down the road he came across a dead lizard, a frog and then a dog. It was his lucky day. The lizard was very old and covered in flies. Fortunately there was a slight breeze so Dam couldn't smell anything.

When he arrived at the Agricultural Department it was midday, the sun was blazing down and the Agricultural people were off to lunch. They'd be back in one hour. Dam waited around. Flies began landing on the boot of his car and he began to feel hungry. He looked longingly over at the car boot and told himself not to take another bite of the apple. After all he had draped all the dead animals across it to stop himself from doing so. Watching the flies feverishly trying to get in the boot made Dam feel hungrier and made him want to get in the boot as well.

Eventually he came out of the shadows and walked over to his car. Clouds of flies were about him and as he bent down to lift up the boot he wondered why it was that anything could be attracted to dead bodies so much. But then he was intent on tasting his apples again and soon forgot about the cuisine of flies.

The boot was stuck. Just near the lock was a piece of dead thing sticking out and this was jamming the boot. Dam said damn as he fought with the flies and then with the lock. Damn he said again as he realised he'd swallowed a fly and they were banging into his eyes. After a while he found he could squash them with his eyelids.

He sat in the car with a thousand flies and wondered what to do. Finding a large oily rag he draped it over his head and tried the lock on the boot once again. This time he bent the key!

"Oh no!" he said as he straightened the key in his teeth. "Nobody bites like Dam," he said as he sat back in his car chewing the key.

He draped the rag over his head again and found a screwdriver inside the car. As he was bending over poking the screwdriver in the boot a police car drove up alongside. Dam removed the oily rag and left it around his neck like a scarf and smiled his yellow teeth smile at the policeman before his face disappeared behind a swarm of flies.

"I've locked my apples in the boot with two dead cats, one dead lizard, a frog and a dead dog!" he said swallowing flies.

The officer got out of his car but soon got back in coughing and spluttering as he too began swallowing flies. Dam thought the officer looked like a fly with his dark glasses on.

Dam got back into his own car. He was alone, he didn't know what to do.

His mind dozed off but soon woke up as his head crashed down on the steering wheel. He felt like he'd slept for days! He turned around and studied the back seat and decided to get into the boot that way.

He removed the back seat with some difficulty then took out the panel which was the back of the boot. As he was taking it out he noticed an arm of something dead and then he saw the maggots.

There were maggots all over the boot, they were coming into the back of the car at a great pace. Dam's apples were there too, not dead but very much alive. He climbed into the boot and squelched about in dead things. It was dark and cramped and very gloomy! He tried to wrestle with the lock again from the inside and made several loud bangs with the screwdriver. Just then somebody tapped on the boot. Dam tapped back.

"Are you alright?" came a voice. They tapped again and Dam tapped back.

They tapped again and Dam tapped back. Then he called out,

"It's alright. I just woke up and I'm covered in maggots!"

Whoever it was went away, perhaps the flies drove them off. Dam was on his hands and knees now, he arched his broken ribs and pushed against the boot and, bang, it flew open. Dam stood up in his boot, he was foul and stinking, flies clustered around his eyes and ran up his nose. His fingers had maggots in between them. He looked like a dead man or road-kill risen from the grave. Several passers-by looked twice and began to run!

Dam smiled at them and waved as flies soon blacked out his teeth.

He stepped out onto the road and scratched around for his apples. He found them amongst the road-kills and heaved them out coughing as he did. Placing them on the ground he rubbed them with the oily rag. Then rubbed himself a little and said,

"Wait till they see what I've got!" He closed the car and in a cloud of flies ascended the few steps to the Agricultural Department.

The building was closed and a sign said 'Air Conditioning please close the door.' Dam quickly opened the door and put the apples inside. Then he began to scare the flies away on the outside by waving his arms and legs around furiously. He made a dash to the door, opened it and in his haste banged into the edge of it before it closed. This allowed hundreds and thousands of flies to enter and gave Dam a very sore fat lip. He picked his apples up and wondered if he smelt alright as he approached the counter pursued by a large black cloud of flies. Fortunately the people serving were all back from lunch and Dam could not help realising that they were extremely well prepared for his visit. One of the gentlemen behind the counter had a bee-veil on, the other had a hat which had hundreds of bobbing corks hanging down around his face and the other man had a can of insect repellent in his top pocket which kept spraying continuously. Dam held his breath.

"We've been watching you!" The man in the bee-veil said.

"You're the bloke with the big apples aren't you?"

Dam thought that was pretty obvious as the apples were sitting on the counter in front of them! Flies began falling out of the sky and Dam's eyes and bruised lip felt the sting of insect repellent. He was being sprayed. He put his fingers on his nose.

"These are extraordinary!" said the man with the insect repellent and added,

"We'll need to photograph these, weigh them and take a mould off them."

Dam said,

"Hang on," and raced outside where he exhaled through his fat lip which vibrated and made a noise like a horse. The three men heard the noise and looked at each other. Dam took a large gulp of air and raced back in. He stood there looking at the men expecting them to say something but they expected Dam to say something. Dam raced outside again and exhaled like a horse, took a breath and raced back in.

"Are you alright" came a familiar voice. Dam nodded then raced outside again. When he came back in the men had walked off. They had taken their bee-veil and hat and insect repellent away and were talking in a back room.

Dam called out hello before he raced outside again, then came back in. His apples had gone!

"Where are my apples?" he said.

"They are being examined," came a reply from the room. "Come back in one hour."

Dam made horse noises all the way to his car. He drove down to the river puffing and panting. The maggots were under his feet as he drove. When he reached the water he waded in, clothes and all but he forgot to wash his face. He swam about thinking about his apples. He sat in the sun to dry off.

"Good road kills!" He said to himself as he admired the clouds of black flies on the windscreen. When he thought an hour was up he drove back to the Agricultural Department. Dam never kept the time on him, he never wore a watch. When he arrived back he found the door had a 'Closed' sign on it.

Dam said damn as he realised he was late and that he'd have to come back in the morning.

Reluctantly he drove home. He emptied the car of road-kills and hosed it out and cleaned it. He went to the bathroom, showered and put some clean clothes on.

That night he dreamt he was a huge ant dressed in battle dress. He was standing on top of a huge round green mountain and up the sides of it were coming armies of maggots with large teeth. Dam was jamming match sticks in their mouths so they couldn't bite and then pushed them off with a broomstick.

Suddenly he realised he was not alone. Turning to the side he saw the very Slow-nurse beside him. She was helping him push the maggots off. Then, much to Dam's dismay she began kissing him. But then to his horror she began tickling him!

Dam woke early and first thing drove into town to the Agricultural Department. When he arrived he went straight up to the front desk.

"Excuse me, I bought a large apple in yesterday and I would like to know if you have finished with it?" he asked.

"What apple?" came the reply.

"My double apple," exclaimed Dam.

"Oh that has gone down to the newspaper," he was told.

Dam raced off in his little smelly car and charged up to the newspaper Head Office.

"Excuse me," he said. "Do you know where my large apples are?"

"Oh they have gone down to the bakers shop."

"Really!" cried dam as he raced out, bruising his lip on the automatic door again. He jumped in his little smelly car and was off down the road.

When he reached the bakers he saw a huge apple pie on the counter.

He was so shocked he held his breath.

"Where are my large apples?" he cried leaning over the counter.

"Oh," he was told, "is that yours?" said the lady pointing to the apple pie.

Poor Dam looked down at his apple. It had been skinned, boiled and baked. The very worst thing imaginable one could do to an apple! Dam picked it up and let out a huge sigh which sounded like a horse.

"Oh! Oh!" he cried. "My apples! There are a thousand road-kills in this."

"We were told to bake it for a Mr Diligent."

"Oh thank you," said Dam the tears welling in his eyes.

"That's not fair!" he said to himself later.

So he drove back to the Agricultural Department determined to get to the core of the problem.

"Oh, Mr Diligent your apples are out the back," a man said.

"What?" said Dam holding his breath again as he began to have visions of tasting his apples once more. He was led out the back and there on a table were Dam's huge apples, complete – large and green. Dam flicked them and put a large hole in the side of one! They were made of plaster! Dam exhaled like a horse.

"My apples!" he cried, resting his hand on the good one.

"These are to be photographed by the newspaper and they want you to go down and have your photograph taken." The man said. Dam had no choice.

On the way out he noticed two huge apple cores in a waste paper bin.

"My apples!" he said holding them up. "Sharks and rats!" he said as he put them in his pockets but they were so big they hung out like road-kills.

Outside he paused then went back and asked, "Where are the three people who work in here?" He was told all three were sick.

"Apple poisoning?" asked Dam "or road-kill diarrhoea?"

Dam had great difficulty carrying the cast of his apples down to the newspaper.

In his little smelly car again he ran over another cat which he threw in the boot. At the newspaper he was photographed holding his apple casts up in front of his chest. The caption on the picture read, 'Dam Big Apples!'

He found it hard to smile and in the picture it looked like he had myriads of dead flies in his eyes. Dam left the cast there for he was told that it was to be put in a museum somewhere and it would be called the 'Diligent Apple.'

Dam went home and hung the apple cores up above his kitchen window so he could save the seeds and plant another tree. Each core was as large as his head. It took him four days to eat the apple pie and six days to get rid of it from his body! In the end he had to confess the pie was delicious.

Days later as he sat on the veranda and looked down to the apple tree he noticed a part of the tree was bending down. Could it be another apple?

Surely he couldn't have missed seeing it. He ran down the slope and looked up.

Sure enough there was a huge single apple on the tree! The size of a basketball!

Dam could barely contain himself. He raced up to the tree and began shaking it. Then he fetched a long stick but that was too short. He began to throw sticks up at it but that didn't work either.

"I know," he said as he lay down beneath it and pretended to go to sleep with one eye open. Quite soon there was a whooshing noise and the apple came hurtling down towards him. But Dam being diligent jumped up and caught it before it hit the ground.

Now Dam is thoroughly sick of apples. If anyone mentions apples to him he turns green and begins to feel ill. Dam's apple tree has become quite famous though and each year the local baker buys all his apples. Generally there is a fight to get to the apples first and Dam only eats a tiny mouthful of apple pie. He takes a very small bite of a bit.

28

Dam Plays with Science

Dam had a BA and a Dip Ed, a P. H. Dilli-D and was a Professor of The Invisible Circuits as he had achieved the highest scientific distinction he could and that was a Dock-door-it (doctorate) from the Head Universally known as the Great Circles of Learning which was another organisation he'd established in the Verifiable Realms rooms of the country's highest dictatorial establishment…long ago.

He had done all this in order to delude others while escaping the 'chromosomal soup' of normality as he called it.

He had suffered the trauma of his Natural body for long enough. Now his ultimate pleasure was the Inter-planetary Buzz and his Small-screen which he could program to kept his artificial hormones alive.

He had been to other planets in the Milky Way Galaxy but he'd decided to remain on earth because of its diverse repository of DNA, which was a library of colossal proportion, necessary for his chromosomal soup-kitchen program of seeding the solar system with earth's genes.

He mused that even with his unique attributes he still needed to eat lunch.

He took his Body-bus down to the ground floor and set his controls on 'Hover.' Holes opened in his feet and he floated across the road using the Terrified program.

He had to move like this as he had so many wires attached to his body at every point which was exposed to the air. The oxygen on earth was being produced underground from great reservoirs of recycled water. The sunlight burnt his retina and the clouds were always red. His thick black glasses bore down heavily on his nose as he raised them to sneeze. He was one of only a few men left on the planet. He was worth his weight in bosons.

Years ago when earth was young, the same as Dam, he had developed a system of robotic health care which produced nano-bots or small electrical devices which could infiltrate cells. These could determine one's destiny for if they found themselves in a DNA they disapproved of they could target that DNA and change its genome to produce insects, worms, or other parasites in the human host. Parasites which would slow the creature down and stop it reproducing.

This was for the benefit of all humanity as it assisted the long term goal of eugenics and population control.

Dam had personally over-seen the early experiments and had since pulled the trigger, as it were, on all those DNA he considered were 'unnecessary eaters' as he called them.

These were people which Dam thought were ugly. For instance since Dam's nose was large he liked people, especially women, with large noses. And since his feet were also large he tended to prefer women with large feet.

This 'Robotic Health Care' was initiated by nano-bots which were small polarised particles which could link up using various types of radiation to form machines. They could be programmed externally to distinguish between male and female. They could also program artificial intelligence.

Since Dam liked women with big feet, no hair and large noses many men with these features were slowly phased out by the invisible circuitry of the nano-bots. This allowed him to pick and choose whichever woman he wanted.

But something in Dam's life was missing. He rarely fell in love anymore because if he did his Small-screen monitor began to flash red and that meant danger. Once it went red one had thirty seconds to change before one's ejector- knees went off automatically and if one was unlucky and unable to get outside one could be blasted into the ceiling!

Dam had studied all aspects of love and decided that if there was one thing which lowered intelligence, it was love. He had been in that position long ago and still remembers the time when, out of shear ignorance, he had to eat his soft horse-hair toupee which fell into his soup while he was courting a lady at a dinner party.

True humans were capable of what was known as 'Higher Adoration' however that was only obtainable after reaching the age of one thousand and then one had to apply to the government or miss out. Applying for the 'Higher Adoration Package' allowed one to become eligible to go in the prize for the Inter-planetary Buzz competition which was exactly what it said. This prise was only available to employees of the government who had worked for over five hundred years and who had had government Small-screen monitors fitted.

Dam was such a person and tried every evening to programme his Small-screen dial under his artificial Belly-flap to the right frequency. Women had this option available to them as well. Though often they were programmed by other special women who came from a star called Serious.

Dam's hormones dropped off years ago. They were only good for silly times. Now Dam had the option of Inter-planetary Buzz which the old hormones never had.

Suddenly Dam's false teeth began misbehaving again and started clanging about in his mouth. The same as a dog which has mange and feverishly mauls its fur. This was an indication that he still had negative reserves left over from his Natural state.

He reached for his gyrocoptic beanie which had fridge magnets all around the edge of it which automatically circumnavigated his scalp every five minutes. The ions in the magnets straightened the nano-bots and forced them to march out of cells and into blood vessels. He slept with this device on as he believed his nose was long enough and he did not want to attract too much attention to himself. Unlike the old days when he had to sleep at least eight hours, now with his gyrocop he only slept for one hour. However the beanie needed to have the polarity of the magnets reversed each night otherwise a severe headache ensued the next day which sometimes required electric shock treatment to alley.

The other thing which he didn't like about growing old was the ringing in his ears. He had designed a strong magnet and put two of them on either side of his head. He would then stand in a bucket of warm salt water and rotate the magnets using electric drills. He experimented to see if the hairs in his cochlea, in his middle ear, would stand back up and behave themselves and keep quiet.

This device had no effect whatsoever. In fact Dam cannot even remember doing the experiment. His deafness was just old age.

This day Dam was out looking for a worm-hole. No other hole would do.

With some worm-holes one could not tell if it was there until one was in it.

And then it was a ride back or forward whichever way one wanted to travel.

Dam went forward once and frightened some people in a room by telling them about their past. They were as confused as he was and offered him some 'Kidney Function Reverse Osmotic Reductant Stimulator' Dam said no thank you and switched over to 'Big Nosed Planet Finder' and 'Big Foot Disease' before he would drink anything.

On the Big Nosed Planet, Dam found he was not noticed as much as he was on earth, for his features blended the same as everybody else's.

Dam liked to be anonymous. He didn't like people rushing out of shops saying, 'There he is!' He liked the thought of spending his old age looking for interesting worm-holes, for he liked the thrills of the Inter-planetary Buzz.

Dam spent his time deluding others and spreading his germs throughout the universe. Since earth was a vicious place beset by this insidious learning he sanctified such revelry which he proudly explained, was the heritage of the earth.

29

Dam Paints a Building

Dam was painting the outside of a building and using a boson's chair which is a small seat that goes up and down. To move up all he had to do was pull on the rope a little and to go down he had to release the rope slightly. He was always very careful to make sure the rope was secure because if he didn't he'd begin to go down slowly, very slowly, according to the amount of paint in the paint tin which was his counter-balance.

Dam began from the top of the building and working his way down as the weight in the tin grew less and less, his own body weight allowed him to be let down.

As he passed the various floors he watched the people inside going about their business. It was a very tall building and Dam was intrigued to see just how many people worked there.

One day he noticed a person carrying a large mail bag. This person visited every desk picking up letters and delivering them. The next day Dam saw the same person on the next floor doing the same thing. He realised then that the person must deliver and pick up mail all the way down to the ground floor forty stories below.

Dam had written a beautiful poem and a letter to his girlfriend Lilly and needed it posted. Since he started work early in the morning and couldn't get to a post-box he tried to catch the mailman's attention by banging on the glass with his tin opener. As he was tapping away the opener accidentally fell in the paint. The mailman was moving rapidly through the building so Dam put the lid on the paint tin and began to use the tin to bang on the window, to attract his attention.

Nobody looked up. Dam had the letter in his teeth and was holding the paint tin in his two hands. He banged again quite hard and the lid of the tin flew off and a large splash of paint lifted itself out of the tin and landed in his face.

Dam was temporally blinded. He carefully put the tin down and wiped his eyes. The letter was covered in paint too. He wiped it and held it between his knees. He looked down below him and could just see the paint lid falling like a butterfly and then as a big white speck on the ground below. He was quite a mess. He had paint all over his hair and his forehead it was even around to his ears.

"What we do for love," he said to himself and resumed painting. A slight wind had sprung up and was growing stronger. As he was working away he noticed a lady quite close to the window. When she saw Dam she waved and he thought she may be able to help post Lilly's letter. Dam picked it up and pointed to it. The woman understood Dam's intention and came closer and pointed to the letter then to herself. Dam nodded and smiled. The woman tried to open the window but it was jammed. Dam gripped the outside of it and they both pulled and pushed.

All of a sudden the window flew open and Dam was pushed backwards.

Somehow the paint tin managed to stay upright but the brush was knocked out of its holder and fell thirty three stories to the ground. Then Dam like a pendulum swung back and came right inside the building above the woman. This time the paint tin did fall off and the woman was covered in white paint!

"Oh! I am...sorry!" Dam said as he swung from inside to outside. He flicked the letter through the window but it landed face down in the paint!

A gentleman ran over to shut the window as flecks of paint were blowing all through the office. Dam was being blown in and out and crashed into the window. He left white hand and cheek marks all over the glass. Luckily he had another tin of paint with him but no way of opening it. He knew where his tin opener was it was inside the building with Lilly's letter.

Dam had to get back inside. He tapped on the glass. But the people inside shook their heads and pointed to the floor. Dam pointed to the tin opener and then his new tin of paint. One man bent down and picked up the tin opener wiped it and put it on the window sill. Presently some people came in with a mop and a bucket. Meanwhile the white woman had disappeared. Dam tied his new tin of paint to the counter balance rope.

He watched his letter being swished this way and that with the mops.

He tapped on the glass and pointed to the letter and then at himself. The men shook their heads as if to say,

"Yes we know you caused this mess!"

Dam tapped again and indicated that he wanted the window open. The men looked the other way and the office workers ignored him too. Dam began to scrape the paint off the window pane with his finger nails, it still hadn't dried. The wind was growing ever stronger and the swing he was on began to move in and out and twist a little.

Presently a man with snow white hair entered the room and luckily, thought Dam, he was carrying a paintbrush in his hand. He came over to the window and pointed to the paintbrush and at Dam and then at his own head. Dam bit his bottom lip. The man then tried to open the window but couldn't. Perhaps the paint had glued it shut? Some other men in the room jumped up shaking their heads and tried to stop the man from opening the window.

Dam held onto his ropes and swayed in and out, he pushed himself off the wall with his feet. As he watched he saw the man with the paintbrush grow angrier and angrier. Then suddenly the man jabbed one of the other men in the eye with Dam's paintbrush. It was a rather large paintbrush and half the man's face became white.

Dam could not do anything but sit and watch as the man with the paintbrush began painting people. Quite a number of people tried to restrain him and quite a few of them had been painted! Eventually the man with the paintbrush seemed to have won and the whole room was standing around him many white faced.

The man tried again to open the window but it was still jammed and Dam realising the fellow was a little angry began pulling on his ropes in order to go up. Just as he was nearly out of sight the window flew open. The man had kicked it!

Dam tried to hasten his retreat but the man dropped the paintbrush on the floor, stood up on the window sill and grabbed Dam's legs! Poor Dam was rudely pulled from his seat and was lucky to hang on to his paint tin and the seat at the same time and prevent the boson's chair from rising or falling.

"Ah!" cried the man below him and

"Argh!" cried Dam above. Both men swung out from the building and back again. Dam could not either go up or down and his arms were under a lot of strain. The man below was swinging freely as he'd lost his foot hold on the window sill. Then a brave man with a white face from inside the office jumped up on the window sill and was reaching out for the other man's legs. But since the other man was kicking wildly he accidentally kicked the brave man in the face and he fell back inside on the small crowd which had gathered.

Then another man with half a white face jumped up on the window sill and reached out. This time he caught a leg and pulled the angry man back to the window sill where he should have been able to let go of Dam's legs but didn't! He kept hold of Dam's trousers instead. The man gave Dam's pants a very hard tug and poor Dam was exposed! Fortunately he was just a little higher than the window but everybody could see his lower half!

Dam climbed up onto his seat again and covered himself with his wet paint rag and crossed his legs. He began to haul himself up and as he approached the other window above he found lots of people looking down at him.

Dam was feeling extremely embarrassed as he moved slowly up in front of them. They all stopped working and silently watched him rising. When he was half way up he noticed a man with a white head enter the room carrying a paintbrush. Dam could not believe it. He stopped pulling on the rope and watched as the man came over to the window. Dam fearing the worst began to rapidly untie knots and lower himself double fast. As he passed the floor below he noticed that everybody had gone to lunch and there on the window sill was his tin opener and his pants. Quick as a flash he pushed off from the wall and swung in through the window where he grabbed his tin opener and his pants.

He lowered himself another three floors and stopped to put his pants on.

He was just tying the tin opener on its piece of string when, "smash!" his paintbrush landed flat on the seat beside him. Dam looked up and saw nothing but blue sky. The wind had died down and he had all he needed to continue working. He opened the lid of the new paint tin and was about to brush some paint on when he remembered the letter. Slowly, very slowly he began to haul himself back up three floors.

As he approached the floor where he last saw his letter, he peeped over the window sill.

The floor was deserted. Dam leapt over the sill and was inside looking everywhere; under tables, in baskets, on benches everywhere but he couldn't see the letter anywhere.

As he was looking under a small table the door flung open and in walked his boss and another man. They closed the door behind them.

"Really Mr Whitewash, he has caused a considerable amount of damage and he keeps flicking paint everywhere!"

"He's my best worker" said Mr Whitewash and added, "They don't call him Dam Diligent for nothing!"

"He's here," said the other man looking out the window. "I hope he hasn't fallen off! They told me he was looking rather ill the last time he passed the window."

Dam crouched down, he didn't want to be seen. He was sure the letter wasn't on that floor anymore, maybe it had been posted after all?

Just then there was a knock on the door and a woman said hello.

"It's Lilly. Come in! Come in!" Dam bumped his head on the table and suddenly six legs were right beside him.

"Lilly!" thought Dam. "Her name is Lilly too and she has the letter!"

Dam wondered if he should reveal himself but decided not to when he heard her say,

"I'd like you to pay for a new dress. It cost me $500."

Dam was horrified. He held his breath. Soon other people began to enter the room and gradually all the workers came back in. Eventually Lilly, Dam's boss and the other man went outside.

The room soon became full of other people. At least nobody came close to his table. But somebody went over to the window and saw Dam's seat hanging there. They looked over the side.

"Wonder where he went?" they said and shut the window. Gradually the office resumed work and when each person was occupied Dam arched his back, lifted the table up and like a crab crawled over to the window. Nobody heard him, slowly he began to raise his head between the wall and the table. When he was high enough to see exactly where he was he turned around and came face to face with three people.

"Hello," they said. "Have you lost something?" Dam received such a shock he bobbed back down. But one of the men crouched down to Dam's level and seeing Dam had found his pants said, "It's alright, you're properly dressed, you can come out now."

Dam coughed a bit and smiled. Some other legs appeared around the table and a few heads looked under. Dam crawled out.

"I was just looking for my letter" he said. "It was addressed to Lilly, err not your Lilly, my Lilly."

"We haven't seen your letter. A lot of papers were ruined by your paint, they are still being cleaned downstairs on floor twenty three."

"Oh," said Dam as he tried to open the window. "Thank you." Dam struggled with the window eventually it flew open and knocked the hanging seat.

Dam had forgotten to tie his paintbrush on and it fell off again and fell to the ground! But that wasn't all; the paint tin did a dramatic wobble and a great slurp of paint fell to the ground as well!

"Oh no!" cried Dam as he sat back down on his hanging chair feeling somewhat like a naughty child. He hesitated for a moment wondering whether to go up or down. He thought that maybe he should take the lift down and retrieve his paintbrush but then he thought he might run into Mr Whitewash so he thought he should lower himself down using the boson's chair instead and look for his letter on the twenty third floor.

Dam began to untie the knot with the intension of lowering himself down. Just as he'd finished a man with a white face appeared at the window. He was holding Dam's paintbrush! He was pointing at it then at Dam. Dam smiled and nodded and made ready to make a quick exit if the man was angry. The window was opened and Dam held himself away from the wall with his legs. The man said,

"Did you drop this?"

"Oh, Mr Whitewash!" said Dam. "No I didn't, somebody else did and I'm terribly sorry. I haven't been able to work all day, people keep throwing my paint around!"

"Well," Mr Whitewash said, "If you weren't so diligent I'd fire you!"

"I'm sorry," said Dam.

Dam was given his paintbrush back and told to get to work.

He sat there above the world, his nostrils were full of paint. He looked at the horizon and then at the immense white building. He was swaying in and out like a fly on a piece of string. White clouds were scudding across the sky in the western sphere and a long, long way off he could see the silver gleam of the ocean. He gave a big sigh.

Dam dipped the brush in the paint and began to brush the wall.

But something in him made him realise that he didn't really like painting buildings. He moved the brush this way and that however his mind was not in it. He wanted an adventure; he wanted to explore the world. As he sat there being swayed by his own heartbeat he began to think about Lilly and her letter.

It had disappeared. His thoughts lay somewhere in a waste-paper basket covered in paint. Today he had somehow managed to paint ten people including himself. He gave a great yawn and try as he might he could not stay awake and soon fell into a deep sleep.

As he slept he dreamed he was on a giant white sheet of ice and in the sky was a great shimmering display of colour. The colour moved and rippled and changed according to which way Dam moved his head. He was so cold his teeth kept making a racket chattering and it was that noise which somehow frightened him for he could not see anything in the whiteness. Then he saw a polar bear in the distance coming towards him. Dam had nowhere to go and as the great lights in the sky lit up he could see that it wasn't a bear after all but Lilly with a hot water bottle!

Dam woke up, it was night time. The lights in the building had gone out and he was suspended in blackness. Way down below him he could see the tiny lights of motor cars as they sped along the streets. Dam's teeth were chattering it was freezing. He quickly pulled himself up to the roof but found the roof door was locked. There was an icy wind on the top of the building so he had to go back down. He lowered himself down to the fateful window and tried to prize it open with his tin opener. Miraculously it opened and he climbed in.

It was dark inside and he stumbled and bumped into chairs and tables as he made his way to the lifts. He stood in the lift and pressed some buttons, nothing happened. He felt around the walls for a light switch and found one. Dam found himself standing in a broom cupboard. On the floor were lots of tins of paint.

He walked around and found the lifts but they were not working, so he went and found the stairs and began walking down.

Down and down he went in the blackness as though he was descending into the bowels of the earth. The stairs turned corners twice for every floor. Half way down he began to feel giddy so he sat down for a little while. As he was sitting there he started thinking of Lilly and all of a sudden he wanted to write her a letter and a poem. Dam leant his head against the cold concrete walls and thought that if he went home he'd still be giddy and also it would probably be daylight when he arrived and he'd have to come back to work. Now he felt alright as though he'd had a good sleep so Dam, being diligent decided to return to his boson's chair and resume work.

Up and up he went as though he was ascending into the realms of heaven.

On the way up he thought how wonderful it would be to watch the sunrise from so high. He also wished he could write a poem on the side of the building to Lilly. When he reached the broom cupboard he looked at the tins of paint and found to his delight that they were a bright orange pink. He took three tins and placed them on the window sill. He replaced his tin of white paint with one of the coloured tins and began to haul himself up the side of the building on his hanging seat.

Dam began to paint. He worked harder than he'd ever worked before and quite soon all the paint was gone. He fetched the two other tins and by the time the first glimmer of dawn was appearing above the horizon those tins were empty too.

As he was panting he thought about Mr Whitewash, his boss and if he'd like what Dam had painted and thought that if he didn't Dam didn't mind if he was sacked.

The sun came up as a bright red ball and gleamed on the freshly painted surface. What Dam had painted could be seen from kilometres around for it was huge. He climbed back through the window and put the empty tins back in the broom cupboard then he resumed painting his white paint.

As the workers arrived Dam noticed they all seemed happy and some said

"Hooray!"

During the day a helicopter flew very close to the building but Dam kept his head down and kept painting. At about lunch time Dam grew hungry and began to run out of paint so he hauled himself up to the top of the building to get more white paint. At the top of the building he met Mr Whitewash just coming up.

"Dam!" he said "It's fantastic! You've created a masterpiece! You're a muralist! Everybody in the building is talking about it. And you know how you ruined Lilly's dress - well she's decided not to ask us for money!"

"Oh, oh!" said Dam, "I thought you'd sack me!"

"No way, you're unbelievable!" said Mr Whitewash and added,

"I can't believe how honest you've made me feel."

Dam puffed his chest up and smiled.

"Muralist!" he repeated and he began to have visions of large paintings on all the tall buildings in the city.

Dam caught the lift down and bought some lunch. When he was on the ground he noticed flecks of white and pink paint all over the pavement.

Nobody seemed to care. People were walking by with their heads looking upwards and then Dam turned around too and looked up at what he'd painted. And there on the side of the building was a gigantic bright pink heart. It was perfectly symmetrical and below it in huge letters were the words, "Lilly I Love You."

30

Dam and the Sky

Dam was trapped beneath the sky. He began to feel claustrophobic. He felt like an ant upon which the sky was falling. The clouds had come down and were scraping the mountains and the trees. He noticed this because he knew they were heavier for they had been spraying metals in the atmosphere to mechanise the weather for many years. Everywhere he went great storms would brew in the clouds about him and the lightning would flicker from his fingers. His eyes had the piercing qualities of lasers and his heart was an earth-moving machine. But he was not happy, he needed to fly. He needed to spread his wings between the planets and the stars. He needed love.

He'd been to the computer shop and they gave him goose bumps at a price. He went to the supermarket and they sold him toxic soap and water which came from a plastic bottle. He went to the horse-piddle (hospital) and they told him to drink bottled water and gave him needles for breakfast and test tubes for his babies. He went to the bank and they asked him how much he wanted for his hair! He had nothing but his bag of bones to sell…cheap.

Thin, starving, and alone. Dam needed to fly!

He went to watch the football and they trod on his toes and made him feel like a deflated football-bladder. He went to the airport and the church, they told him to sit and wait. He went to the graveyard and looked at the book where his parents' names were written long ago.

At night he dreamt he was flying. He took her in his arms and together they flew into the deep dark universe looking for love. She tried to help him find what he wanted but he would not be pleased.

Dam began directing storms with his fingers. He pointed at the sky and moved his arms around and great clouds formed and lightning flashed in his eyes. He did not want to save earth anymore. Everybody was an ant and they were all fighting amongst themselves.

Dam needed peace and love. He wrecked the earth with his stare. He looked at the sun and threatened to blot it out of the sky as it was an engine of intelligence and gave life to seeds and people who only fought amongst themselves and suffered because they, each and every one, was like himself who could not find peace. Dam had become a machine like the sun and wanted to be human again.

She told him not to worry. He was too thin to care about it - his bag of bones the same as hers. They were both earth bound and it made Dam sad.

All the people on earth were only interested in money. They were running so fast for what? The fish and the birds were all dying. Dam had given his ideas to them and they had pillaged his thoughts and used them to control others.

His thoughts only gave energy for their machine. Dam would not be controlled!

All he wanted to do was dig in his garden and fish in his seas. But he had to pay money now and it was love which had caused the problem. Even though that is what Dam wanted he knew it would only make more children. And there were too many people on the planet. Even the insects were dying – the soils washing away.

Lilly and Dam went for a holiday.

They brought a plane ticket and a train ticket. Then they walked and walked to the edge of the earth. Even Dam did not know where they were going. Eventually they came to a small stream full of letters of the alphabet.

They saw the alphabet from all the nations mixing together in the same water.

They followed the letters downstream and watched in the waterfalls as the letters came together and made words. When the water was still, the words broke up and were indecipherable.

They followed the river to the edge of the earth and found where it began to fall into the sky. And looking up they could see that the whole sky was like a huge book covered in words. Dam pointed his lightning fingers at the words and they all began to melt and fall like rain. Letters came down the more he waved his arms. Until a great flood of graffiti was all around.

They both sat down on a small hill. But Dam sat on something and stood up again quickly.

Bending down he found a small piece of metal in the shape of a sphere.

He put it to his ears and was delighted to find he had good reception. He pressed it a few times and it changed language. Finally he found English and they both sat down to listen. It was a radio broadcast and fortunately for Dam the news was about to begin.

However the news was not good - more fighting. When it was over they both looked at each other and knew it was no good.

Dam held her close and checked her transmission. He pressed her a few times then pressed his ejector-knees and they both shot into orbit and circled the earth three times before venturing off again into the plasmoid realms.

Printed in the United States
By Bookmasters